VARYING DEGREES
OF
HOPELESSNESS

VARYING DEGREES
OF
HOPELESSNESS

~~Lucy Ellmann~~

For Avril,

from the depths of

hopelessness,

HAMISH HAMILTON · LONDON

HAMISH HAMILTON LTD
Published by the Penguin Group
Penguin Books Ltd, 27 Wrights Lane, London W8 5TZ, England
Penguin Books USA Inc., 375 Hudson Street, New York, New York 10014, USA
Penguin Books Australia Ltd, Ringwood, Victoria, Australia
Penguin Books Canada Ltd, 2801 John Street, Markham, Ontario, Canada L3R 1B4
Penguin Books (NZ) Ltd, 182–190 Wairau Road, Auckland 10, New Zealand

Penguin Books Ltd, Registered Offices: Harmondsworth, Middlesex, England

First published 1991
1 3 5 7 9 10 8 6 4 2

Copyright © Lucy Ellmann, 1991

The moral right of the author has been asserted

Printed in England by Clays Ltd, St Ives plc

A CIP catalogue record for this book is available from the British Library

ISBN 0-241-13153-7

For my mother

Had we never lov'd sae kindly
Had we never lov'd sae blindly,
Never met – or never parted,
We had ne'er been broken-hearted.

(Robert Burns – 'Ae Fond Kiss')

If of me you sometimes think
    Send me back my knot of pink!

If with me you will unite
    Send me back my knot of white!

If to me your love is dead
    Send me back my knot of red!

If you have another fellow
    Send me back my knot of yellow!

(Edwardian Valentine)

Je chante pour moi-même.

(Georges Bizet – *Carmen*)

The Catafalque

It was not the best place in the world to study Art History. It was not the worst. It did not warrant the superlative degree of comparison. Within its high-ceilinged halls, lurking behind the plaster pillars painted to look like marble, slumped against the shelves of its reportedly estimable library, going up and down in the ancient two-person lift, were the usual degrees of wisdom and foolishness, belief and incredulity, light and darkness, hope and despair. It was Dickensian, in short, and just as one tolerates a lot of nonsense in Dickens, a lot of it was tolerated here.

The acme of Art Historical endeavour was to be received into permanent paid slumber in some outermost reach of the warren-like structure in Purport Place (a dull corner of London's West End, primarily devoted to public baths and private nursing-homes), and therein to skulk unseen by any but the most importunate students professing a lamentable interest in their subject, or lively part-time lecturers unlikely to be invited back next year.

It was an establishment that had long outgrown its usefulness but was far too doddery to care. It was a finishing school in an era when the young no longer wished to be finished off. The Catafalque did not seek to explain its shortcomings. Indeed, Catafalquian explanations so quickly withered outside the sacred confines that it was deemed prudent to air them as little as possible. Oblivious to all else, the Catafalque annually conferred degrees upon individuals who were well able to take their places at any dinner table in the land, and were intent on doing so.

Many of this misguided crowd came, it must be said, from unfortunate backgrounds: at an early age they had been forced to don navy-blue blazers with gold buttons, as well as various articles of clothing constructed out of tweed, with a stylelessness which they and their many authenticated forbears considered attractively aristocratic. Others had won their places beside the Catafalque's stolid shelves through hard work, abject submission to examinations and their results, and the belief that the Catafalque was a distinguished institution dedicated to the advancement of Art History as a respectable academic discipline. Without ado, and often much to their relief, these *ingénues* were soon informed that Art and History were but side-issues in a study that was more concerned with the geographical location and monetary value of two-dimensional antiques.

The Catafalque's learned and esteemed professors were much in demand on TV, having proved their willingness – for a fee (their salaries were not luxurious) – to have their hair coiffed and curled, their cheeks powdered to a fashionable shade of bronze, their lips accentuated, their ears wired, and thus arrayed to mouth on about this or that CRUCIAL painting of the fifteenth, sixteenth, seventeenth, eighteenth or nineteenth century, often whilst walking dottily along a public thoroughfare, nimbly preceded by the camera. This noble task, however, did little to shift the prevailing view throughout Britain that scholars, academics and intellectuals are the dregs of the earth, a weedy and wimpish lot prone to plumpness in the posterior.

As some fridges grow cultures, the Catafalque sprouted talents of sorts. There was the perpetually grumpy Librarian who, having journeyed alone to the limits of human irritability, was able to transmit this state of mind to anyone within range. Countless generations of students wandered the stacks for the whole of their three years without ever realizing that books on Sculpture, American Art, Cave-Painting and other subjects which the Librarian viewed with distaste were all kept hidden somewhere in the basement. He would reveal his system to no one.

There was the Keeper of the Queen's Pictures, of whom the Catafalque was resolutely proud. Sir Humphrey Basilisk's stumbling agedness, misogyny and other Etonian traits thinly disguised a reckless sexual and political past during which he had tunnelled himself a moledom, and thence a knighthood, in MI5. His legendary deceitfulness was considered an asset to the Catafalque, which had pledged itself to promote the fleeting and ephemeral. This cultured edifice was forever traipsing after will-o'-the-wisps.

Despite his many misgivings, Sir Humphrey had authorized in a weak moment the recruitment of one female member of staff (besides the tea-lady in the basement). Angelica Lotus, though saintly and reserved on home-ground, tended to vacation uproariously and rather frequently in Vienna, where she claimed to be doing some sort of research. On her return, she delivered pleasant, unadventurous lectures and was kind to students taking their vivas. Appalled by certain signs of a clandestine zest for life, Lotus's colleagues took comfort in the fact that she was at least past child-bearing age.

Then there was old Splutters. He, bony, balding and perceptibly past his prime, liked to arrive eagerly early in the morning and station himself near the main entrance, where it was possible for this committed pedagogue to leer appreciatively at each new female fledgling in the Art Historical throng. His pointer, during lectures, lingered helplessly over the naked feminine protuberances in the paintings of the Old Masters. That such works were Masterpieces was one of the few certainties of a remote and intangible universe in which Splutters often felt it necessary to qualify his statements with the phrase, 'as it were'. In reaction, as it were, to the fundamental perplexity of his being, as well as to the advent of any provocatively clad student, Splutters was occasionally to be found up a tree in the Gardens behind the Institute, holding an umbrella in one hand and his penis in the other.

By dint of such unceasing efforts to reveal his availability to the opposite sex, Splutters attempted to rival the unrivalled, the unparalleled, Splendid Young Man. A favourite at the BBC and most students' first choice for infatuations, Lionel Syms's suave charm ensured a moist atmosphere of unrequited longing in whatever dingy seminar room he entered. He was fond of giving seminars, during which he alone spoke, smiling beguilingly the while. Three colour-illustrated books already lay on those unyielding library shelves, attesting the Splendid Young Man's precociousness, although he had by now reached the stage when his youth was beginning to be a matter of opinion.

Finally, there was Cragshaw. Mad, weird, idle, shunned and depressed, Dr Cragshaw had long since been awarded his own two-room prefab at the back of the Gardens where, incidentally, he would have commanded an excellent view of the Splutters behind, had he ever opened his blinds. Here, in artificial light and darkness, breathing air that mainly he alone had breathed for years, Cragshaw applied himself assiduously to his internationally recognized, if not exactly acclaimed, examination of Chardin's brushstrokes. By the meticulous perusal of his own close-up photographs of individual brushstrokes, gathered during numerous holidays spent padding myopically around the back-rooms of museums throughout the world, Cragshaw found himself able, more or less, to confirm with some degree of certainty other people's rough estimates of when a particular Chardin painting was painted by Chardin. Known solely for this, Cragshaw was occasionally consulted. He was not an altogether unfamiliar figure at Chardin conferences, where he could always be relied on to fill in with a mumbled slideshow of individual brushstrokes if no one more sensible could be found. Not that Dr Cragshaw was not revered, by a small number of like-minded scholars, for his excess of good English common sense: this accomplishment almost gleamed, as it were, from his slumped and penitential form.

A true product of the Catafalque Institute, Purport Place (he had spent his entire adulthood within its reassuring shadow), Cragshaw had a hearty distaste for the more glaring perversities of modern Art Historical discourse. Questions of artistic intention, social and political influences, aesthetic effects or subjective responses could not have been further from his wholesome, unfettered mind. FACTS (historical and material) were all that concerned him. Leave the rest to arty-farty critics, media junkies, unstructured post-structuralists and gatherings of the Workers' Educational Association in Lewes (he had once given a rather unsuccessful talk there, delineating his *raison d'être* at some length).

Day in, day out (in between gins), Cragshaw studied his snapshots.

Our Heroine

Into this famed and dusty institution came I.

I, Isabel, menstruating, alienated and allergic to nuts.

I, thirty-one years of age and still a virgin.

I, a thirty-one-year-old virgin with a nervous habit of repeating myself.

I, who move fast in the way of all people who have been told they move slowly.

I, a dismal, disenfranchised devotee of the historical romances of Babs Cartwheel.

I, an ageing virgin holding out for Mr Right.

I, who'd had offers but wasn't going to settle for second-best.

I, who had in fact considered these offers improper suggestions.

Insults, really.

I, a shiftless romantic with high hopes for Art History as the career most suited to my acute sensibility and 20–20 vision.

I, Isabel, on a fine autumn day when the sky was creamy blue and something inevitable was bound to happen, entered the Catafalque Institute at an early hour with a few brown leaves.

It was the year one thousand nine hundred and eighty-seven.

The 31-year-old Woman Falls in Love

He was athletic.

He had a masculinity.

His broad shoulders and narrow hips gave him a distinctive physique.

He held seminars and wore red socks.

To hold seminars seemed to indicate a wish to develop a rapport with his students.

The red socks seemed to indicate testosterone.

I swooned in admiration of him.

Along with the rest of my seminar group, 90% of whom were female, youthful, and of riper proportions than I.

Competition for the most spiritual attachment was therefore fierce.

He had a very manly physique.

The 31-year-old Woman Makes a Salad

I was a virgin.

I was thirty-one years old.

I had had no suitors for some time.

And it seemed that all of London had other things to do besides speculate on whom I might marry.

This made sense, as I was not perfectly beautiful.

I was not even remotely beautiful.

My eyes were not translucent.

The sunshine streaking through the kitchen window while I made the salad failed to bring my hair to life.

At least so far as you'd notice.

I was neither spirited nor obstinate.

And my fortune was not large.

In fact it was non-existent.

My father had died before I was born.

We had lived in near poverty ever since.

My father had been a very attractive man, I'm told.

He had a masculinity and was very handsome.

I was determined to marry someone like him.

It had not yet been my destiny to meet my true soul-mate.

But, having read a plenitude of romantic fiction, I was ever hopeful.

And somewhat depressed.

I peeled the mushrooms.

Mushrooms should always be peeled.

One never knows where they've been.

Which is what people say to disguise the fact that they do know where they've been.

They've been in manure.

Mushrooms are grown in manure.

Then we eat them.

Feeling somewhat squeamish about such things, I carried out intensive cleaning operations on all the ingredients for my salad.

All vegetables grow in or near dirt, after all.

It does not really bear thinking about.

While I peeled and scrubbed my vegetables I thought dreamily about the Splendid Young Man at the Catafalque.

He had put 'This is splendid!' at the bottom of my essay.

I wished he would put 'This is splendid!' on MY bottom!

He had such a manly physique.

I sliced the lettuce into very thin slivers.

My mother lumbered in like a pack-mule, festooned with carrier-bags.

My step-father had a bladder problem.

I too had often had to hoist home huge plastic bottles of soft drinks for him.

They were essential to his health.

My mother subsided into a chair, perspiring and panting profusely.

She was exhausted.

She was pooped.

She was plump.

She looked terrible up close.

Her heart was not what it had been.

She should never have married a man so much younger than herself.

Such relationships never work.

9

Our Heroine's Mother Makes an Entrance

She had survived being a teenager during the war and all those desperate dances when you were expected to marry a GI at the least provocation. She had resisted the most tragic entreaties in the most tragic of circumstances, but later on had had some difficulty in extricating herself from a brief entanglement with Isabel's father: he raped her beside a disused railway line. But no one would believe that she had taken a stroll along a disused railway line with someone she did not want to make love to. The police at any rate did not find her distress convincing. The whole story obviously made no sense at all.

For some years she lived a ruined life with an unmarried aunt, and supported Isabel by making hats and cooking school dinners. She found comfort in the company of children. The hats embarrassed Isabel, once she was old enough to study them properly, but her mother compared herself to a brain surgeon: fixing up people's heads. She put her all into those hats. Bits of frill and fluff gave her hope.

She was very fond of Isabel, her worn-looking rape-child, and did not hold the circumstances of her birth against her. She ignored the physical resemblance between the child eating her beans on toast, and the brute who had planted his seed in the gravel beside the tracks. And as the years went by, the memory faded and died.

Later, she formed an alliance with a man much younger than herself, a man with small feet who didn't scare her, a man who earned his living by entering supermarket competitions and the occasional raffle. They presented their marriage to Isabel as a *fait accompli*, as fate in fact. But Isabel questioned it. She missed the big messy bed she and her mother had always shared, which was now made neatly every morning. The flat was full of soft drinks and nasty furniture. And the hats went all to pot: they were a feather here, a scrap of veil there, a miniaturized fruit tottering on top.

Isabel watched in dismay as her mother succumbed to the effects of trying to keep a young man happy and alive. Her coquetry turned into mere clownishness as she got varicose veins and heart palpitations. She became, in short, the sort of woman who has to keep her feet up, wear support hose, and exercise her calf muscles.

The new family went to Beatles films together and sat in brooding silence, baffled by the exultation all around them.

Our Heroine's Step-Father and His Fateful Influence

Alan, my step-father, changed our lives.

I resented him at first.

We had led a very peaceful existence, based on tea and toast, before he came along.

It was an irregular household, for there was no man about.

I hardly knew anyone but my mother, for my great-aunt had left us for the next world when I was three.

But I was perfectly happy.

Alan's arrival meant a lot more cooking and cleaning.

Yet, when my mother's plumpness turned to droop, and her coquetry became mere clownishness, I began to feel for Alan more.

And it was Alan, my step-father, who first showed me how romantic art is.

He was always going to exhibitions.

He bought museum catalogues.

He read art reviews.

He often recited the phrases that had particularly struck him.

For instance, 'The black of a hole is like the flame of a fire.'

But there were others that were equally profound.

'I like to sculpt in soap because it's a proletarian substance. There's a universal need to keep clean.'

'His unassuming pastoral scenes are heroic in their modesty.'

'Franklin has been using ant-hills in his work for the past sixteen years.'

'These crudely welded metal chairs marry plastic expression of pure neurosis with the offer of rest.'

'Poised between describing emotional and social states and creating exquisite abstractions, he uses elongated, roughly triangular plates.'

'The sculpture is characterized by its defiant hold on everyday reality, its desire for a direct confrontation with the viewer and by its unease in the face of interpretation.'

'This piece was inspired by those dolls whose hair grows if you press a button.'

'My paintings are a form of vaginal iconoclasm.'

I found modern art disconcerting at times.

So I decided to concentrate on older art.

I was fascinated by the tradition of artists starving in garrets as they awaited a rich patron.

Artists whose names went unrecognized until after their deaths.

And heiresses forced to paint beautiful pictures in Bohemian surroundings in order to escape the clutches of a mad earl or uncle intent on marrying them for their fortunes as well as for their faultless beauty.

And noblemen who bought paintings because they had fallen in love with the artist's model.

The household was full of lofty ideas of this kind.

Art Historical Romance

I was in a state of some excitement as I approached the Catafalque that delicious spring morning in the year one thousand nine hundred and eighty-eight.

Yes, things had moved on apace.

The day previous to that had been a turning-point in my life.

I was sitting in the cafeteria enjoying some tea and toast after a splendid seminar with the Splendid Young Man.

Suddenly, he appeared behind me and put his arm around my shoulders in a jovial manner!

He asked me if there was anything edible in the cafeteria.

It lasted only a moment, but it was momentous.

The thought flashed through my mind that even being married could not have made us closer than we were at that moment.

I recommended tea and toast to him, and warned him against the tea-cakes.

Before this incident, he had seemed rather reluctant to get near me.

For many months I do not think he even knew my name.

So this had given me a lot to think about, as I approached the Catafalque that delicious spring morning.

Should I have it out with him? I wondered.

Should I confess my feelings for him?

My feeling, for instance, that we were made for each other.

My feeling that he had a very attractive physique and physiognomy.

My feeling that he must be getting sick of all those forward girls who were too young for him.

My feeling that he dallied with them because he had not yet found the love of a good woman.

My feeling that he was looking for something more sincere, more lasting, more secure, more respectable: in fact, A VIRGIN BRIDE.

And my feeling that I could help him with his work.

The thought was tantalizing.

It was enthralling.

It was stimulating.

It was unwieldy.

It was unbearable.

I wondered if I would meet him in the hallway.

This too was tantalizing.

And all the rest.

It was all so exciting that I thought I must calm myself in private before I could possibly encounter the man of my dreams.

The very thought of him gave me digestion problems.

I hurried into a ground floor loo before anyone could see me.

I was just sitting down, feeling very anxious, when someone knocked.

Could it be HIM?

Having seen me flutter by and sensing my distress, had he come to pull me to him and whisper sweet plans for eternity?

Had he come to tell me that we were made for each other?

My saviour, my soul-mate, my destiny, with his slight aura of the divine.

I called my poor dead father to help me.

Feeling soft and feminine and vulnerable, ripe as putty to be moulded in my lover's strong hands, I tremblingly, despairingly, hopefully opened the door.

I was his, the all of me (if required).

Demurely, I lifted my eyes to my master, my guide, my guardian.

Unfortunately, it turned out to be Dr Lotus who had knocked.

I had been recovering myself on the Female Staff Loo, designated in other words for her sole use.

I murmured something by way of apology and hurried off.

Various Objectionable Bits of Our Heroine's Body

People say that if one loves a man, one should tell him.

The trouble is, I deal with rejection badly.

I stutter, go pale, feel faint.

Self-hatred produces in me a number of embarrassing physical manifestations.

My cheeks atrophy, leaving my mouth unable to smile and my eyes unable to close (should I wish to smile and close my eyes whilst being rejected).

I stumble, feel faint, need a sit-down.

I find it difficult to carry the situation off with aplomb.

I, a thirty-one-year-old virgin with rough skin on my heels.

I, a thirty-one-year-old virgin with dark hairs that go every which way on my big toes.

I, with a permanent stain on my left eye from a ping-pong accident in childhood.

I, with my knobbly knees.

I, bony as a goat, with a distended stomach to match.

And hardly any breasts to speak of (should I wish to speak of breasts).

I, whose auburn locks are not brought to life by sunlight.

I, whose eyes do not have a translucence.

I, with moles in unmentionable places.

I, who behave with the perpetual jumpiness of someone who has been told too often that I am a slow eater, a slow reader, a slow walker.

I, who therefore move erratically and eat without pleasure.

I, who have never been allowed to revert to MY OWN NATURAL SPEED.

I, who blush when intimate areas of male and female anatomy, even *vis-à-vis* insects, are mentioned.

I, who sometimes burp and fart.

I, who sometimes (in private) burp, and the other thing, and do not MIND.

I, Isabel!

How could I say to someone, 'I love you'?

Would a normal man be likely to be pleased by this news?!

But I did try to show the Splendid Young Man how much I loved him, just by little things I did.

I wore my best Janet Reger knickers to his classes.

And fingernails.

Fingernails are important.

No man likes a woman with battered fingernails.

And I used my intellect to try to impress him.

I exerted myself in this regard.

I like a man I can argue with.

Seeking his admiration, I threw interesting points at him with increasing frenzy during our seminars together.

It was a duel of words, which was at times stimulating, at others slightly embarrassing.

He often tried to shut me up.

He ignored my quieter utterances entirely.

Perhaps he sensed the dry skin on my heels.

The strange construction of my belly-button.

Could he detect the defects of my knees through the folds of my long, carefully ironed skirt?

Or did he foresee that I might be ill in old age, and he didn't want to have to take care of me?

DID HE HAVE SOME SIXTH SENSE ABOUT HOW UGLY MY BODY IS WHEN NAKED?

Our Heroine in Jeans

I actually look rather good in jeans.

So I rarely wear them.

I don't want to get mixed up with the wrong sort of person.

Men who are only interested in me for my body.

I don't want to settle for second-best.

(I also have nice arms.)

Our Heroine's Strict Notions of Propriety

Dishes should be washed and dried immediately after use.

The drying process should not be left to the natural laws of physics.

It shows a lack of resolve to leave dishes dripping by the sink.

(Also, many people probably have jobs in dish-cloth factories.)

Pink and orange should never be worn together.

Likewise, blue and green.

Newspapers should be refolded to look as if no one has read them.

One should not place cups of tea upon library books.

Mushrooms should be peeled.

Vegetables should be well boiled.

Pasta on the other hand should be *al dente*.

Meat must be carved at the correct angle.

One should not appear over-eager to eat food.

Or to do anything else, for that matter.

But tea and toast can be consumed in any quantity.

This harms no one.

Taps should be run while relieving oneself of bodily wastes, or brushing one's teeth, to disguise disgusting sounds.

Music should be played loudly whilst others are doing the same, to protect them from embarrassment.

Flushing should be thorough, and the toilet inspected to ensure this.

Men should not burp in front of women. (Women should not burp in front of anyone.)

Women should be treated with respect.

It is best to wear trousers when riding a bicycle.

The 31-year-old Woman's Attitude to Relationships

It is amazing what people will settle for.

I saw a couple on a train once.

The woman looked much older than the man.

His name seemed to be Gavin.

Gavin had long hair in a pony-tail.

Gavin had long hair and the responsibility of going for the sandwiches when they're travelling.

Truly pathetic: she, too old for him, crouching over her magazine, while he, merely too hairy, stalking off in search of British Rail sandwiches.

A friend of mine invited me to Sunday lunch with her and her boyfriend and, almost as soon as I got there, he began to weep.

I assumed his rocky emotional state was due to the fact that he was a former fruit-machine addict.

But my friend soon explained that Sunday was their usual day for making love.

I suggested I leave, but she insisted I stay for lunch.

He kept passing by the door of the sitting-room, sobbing.

Soon she was crying too, and trailing up and down the stairs after him.

Finally they both came down and we ate nut roast.

To which I was allergic.

I kept apologizing.

But actually I was thinking, not only do they cry to-gether, but she has to watch him SHAVE every morning.

The thought repulsed me.

Had she no pride?

And then there are those couples who constantly inter-rupt each other, so you don't know who you're supposed to be listening to.

You're bound to offend one or the other.

They speak in tandem but each expects to get your full attention.

These are not at one with each other.

I do not know why so many people settle for second-best.

There were few men for whom I would sacrifice my independence and sense of personal space and identity.

In fact, baring my soul or any other part of myself to a man was for me practically unimaginable.

Even experienced people seemed to encounter numerous hurdles in the search for a soul-mate.

For instance, the woman who wrote this sad letter to a magazine:

> My problem is: MEN. I'll never understand them. Are there any I can trust? I'm twenty-six and met my first boyfriend at seventeen. He was handsome and funny, but stingy. Two years later I met Joe who was funny and bought me presents, but he was not so handsome. After seven months, he tried to strangle me. My next boyfriend was a reliable person, but not very good in bed. After five years, I got bored. All I want is to be married with ten children and an Afghan hound. Is this too much to ask?

Of course, she should never have lost her virginity.

According to Babs Cartwheel, in her 373 treatises on the subject, when the right man appears, he will appreciate finding your virginity intact.

And yet, there was no doubt that my virginity somewhat hampered my own progress in life.

In contrast to the era of high romance, men now find the precious gift of one's virginity a slightly daunting prospect.

I was not particularly attached to my virginity.

I would have given this precious gift to any man I truly loved, whether or not we were yet married.

To be still in possession of one's virginity at the age of thirty-one is an encumbrance.

But I firmly believe that, if one cannot change a man, one must find the right one the first time.

I wanted to choose carefully.

And I had chosen the Splendid Young Man.

He too seemed to be saving himself for that special somebody.

Despite his many admirers, to whom he was invariably gracious and polite.

We were destined for each other.

A woman knows these things.

Why else would I have ended up at the Catafalque, and in his seminar group?

I knew we could be happy together.

He seemed to enjoy tea and toast.

If only he could overcome his shyness, and make clear his intentions towards me.

Mrs Lionel Syms.

Perhaps Ms Isabel Syms sounded more feminist.

Ms Isabel Syms.

Rather striking, I thought.

The Letter 'Q'

One hundred and seventy-eight men had been burnt alive on an exploding oil rig in the North Sea. A so far unidentified sniper had gunned down twenty holiday-makers on a Turkish cruise ship for a so far unspecified reason. The US Air Force had sent the contents of an Iranian passenger plane to Allah. By contrast, the new president of Mexico had just gained office by resurrecting thousands of long-dead voters and persuading them to fill out ballot papers in his favour. A bee disease was spreading across Europe. Whales on the way to their mating-ground were thinking profound thoughts and probably, like us, using only a tenth of their brains. Forty-five children in the Borough of Islington had been beaten up before setting off for school. Car alarms wailed to their owners all over London in deafening expressions of outrage or ennui. And people throughout England and Wales still lay in beds covered with cats. It was a normal day.

Lionel Syms, beaming with post-coital smugness, tickled a crouching girl's neck as he reviewed his notes on Degas. He waited tolerantly as she tied his shoe-laces. He had never learned how to tie shoe-laces properly, and now considered it too late. Sir Humphrey Basilisk elsewhere – though he would happily have been doing up the Splendid Young Man's shoe-laces – searched out a decent position for the black toupee on his eighty-year-old head. Believing that he had found one, he proceeded to search for his teeth, mumbling to himself about the sacrifices one makes for Beauty and Love. Cragshaw, regaining consciousness after a night spent on the floor of his rooms at the Catafalque, noticed that he was running low on gin and telephoned his wife to bring another bottle, feeling for the moment unable to face another brushstroke without it.

Babs Cartwheel had written to the *Daily Telegraph* that morning to extol the pleasures of motoring in France. Besides toy poodles, virgins, beeswax, gypsies and housewives, motoring in France seemed to be one of her pet subjects. 'Why oh why,' she asked, with her indefatigable eloquence, 'can't our roads be made as enjoyable?' As always, she gradually ground to a halt. Splutters, smirking, had read her letter along with everything else in the paper on his way to the Catafalque. His mind needed constant sustenance, even when walking, on account of a surplus of energy and erudition. He was in a particularly good mood that day, for he had been practising the deaf alphabet with his penis in the early hours and had reached the letter 'Q'. His knowledge of the deaf alphabet was just one more facet of the dynamic and wide-ranging scholarship which had won him a permanent position at the Catafalque: he was their expert on historiography, hagiography, iconography and Kant. He was also in love.

She was a mature student.

She stared at him with big blue eyes.

The sunlight shimmered in her hair.

She looked very good in jeans.

He said her splendidly romantic name over and over to himself.

Isabella.

Isabella.

Isabella.

He could hardly bear to imagine the calligraphic intricacies of her pubic hair.

Prancing

Nearing the dull grey building in its dull grey part of a dull grey city on this dull grey day is Pol, and she prances. It is a type of movement not often performed by English women these days. Women used to like themselves more. Before they were assured by feminists that men hate them, women used to prance more. You see them displaying their corset-wear in old magazines. They did not hate themselves. They did not even seem to hate their corsets. They did not mind if their breasts protruded with a lack of premeditation. Everyone was prancing in those days. Now models crouch and slink like girls pretending they haven't reached puberty (perhaps they haven't). They are not supposed to look happy. We are at the anti-climactic turn of a century.

Or perhaps it's just a matter of bad posture.

Pol prances. She wears a tight pink and orange outfit that amply highlights her distinguishing sexual characteristics, her distinguished sexual characteristics – an abundance of unfashionable, unrequired flesh. Her breasts flop about, her nipples are far from erect. She has wide, rounded, ovalled, overlapping hips, complete with a revolutionary number of dimples. Her legs are not sticks. Her arms wobble. And the whole conglomeration is gyrating, caught in the widening gyre, as she prances. A blob of slithering, tremblous matter, Pol moves lustily through space.

Pol's Mother

Pol had always been a nervous naked flame, trying to live. Every fire needs help, or luck. Her mother had loved her carelessly but well, like a well-fed cat is loved. A child's life is so precarious: she was pleased to see Pol grow substantial.

She had not realized her own beauty until she was thirty-eight, when it was beginning to wane. She was determined that Pol would not suffer the same fate. When Pol wanted to wear a bikini at the age of six, her mother refrained from saying that Pol's proud baby stomach, sticking out between the two halves of the swimming costume, did not look sexy. Pol thought it did.

The Seminar

Syms was in fine fettle and full flow. His laces had remained tied for hours. His manly frame paced the room with manful stride, in jeans that called attention to his man-root. The hands clasped earnestly behind the back, the charming frown and the moussed hair all indicated that whatever his next ejaculation might be, it would be well worth inserting in one's notebook. He tossed his head, not only with the intention of displaying his wavy blond curls to better advantage, but perhaps in an effort to dislodge yet another memorable thought from the grey matter encased within.

Twenty eyes followed his movements back and forth, up and down, in and out of the ten feet of available promenading space, and added their assent, were it needed, to his high estimation of himself. Twenty bedroom eyes took him in from head to toe, caressing his every curve, his every lack of curve. Ten heads turned for him, and ten minds tried to hold on to his information for as long as they could.

But there were eleven students in the room, and the eleventh jerked around in her chair, slapped her knees occasionally, let out low grumbles that could no longer be attributed to her digestive tract, and was generally proving an impediment to the smooth running of the seminar group situation. Taking things in hand, as was his wont, Syms turned to the source of the disruption and asked quite kindly, 'Is there a problem of some sort?' Twenty eyes reluctantly transferred their attention from him to the fat girl in the back row.

'You bet there's a problem, buddy.'

'Well, what?' he asked, with manly simplicity.

'Laundry lists! That's what. All you guys ever seem to talk about is when and where and for whom the thing was done, you never talk about the painting itself. The closest you get to talking about the picture is when you're maundering on about the various influences, how this painting looks a bit like that one. The only reason we're sitting through this stuff is that we're all waiting for the day you finally delve into why we have been *moved* by paintings. But you're so scared of feelings like that you'd talk about anything just to avoid talking about them. I've been in this place for six months and I've never heard so much utterly useless data in my life. All you care about is crushing paintings, that is what you do, you sit around covering works of art with peripheral and BORING information like the guy must have painted it in 1885 because he rented a studio and was seen in Paris in May. Here's his bar bill, here's the illegitimate child born nine months later to Marie Louise who lived down the road, here's the washer-woman's testimony. Who cares WHEN the fucking painting was done? Who the hell CARES? I want to talk about the thing itself. It's only of value surely, and worthy of discussion, if the thing in and of itself expresses something, takes the viewer into its own territory, does SOMETHING, something new. Who cares that it's a bit like this or that, if what it really is is NEW? Who cares whether Braque or Picasso did all those crazy collages? THEY didn't. A work of art should be able to subsist without any reference to the painter. If its only appeal rests on the fact that a famous guy painted it, well, what the fuck are we doing? Are we some sort of out-of-date fan club or what?'

'Um, I'm not sure I quite –'

'This is demeaning. I didn't come here to belittle art, and belittle my own intelligence. What we need is art CRITICISM, like literary criticism. Why doesn't art deserve the same kind of attention? When and where a picture was done is only worth even being curious about if you've already figured out WHY it was done. But with you, there's no TIME to discuss the paintings because you're always talking about the laundry!'

This unbelittlable person seemed capable of going on all day. Syms had to do something. 'I see,' he began, with a slow and startlingly handsome nod. 'You think we should be talking about how a picture makes us FEEL. Like, "Ooooh, that Renoir's like a nice blanket, it makes me go all warm and tingly", for instance? Or maybe, "Munch must have been feeling pretty awful when he painted *that*"? Don't you think such a discussion might end up being a waste of time too? Everybody has a different impression. Where do we go from there?'

'So literary criticism is merely boring?'

'Well, I don't think you should throw the baby out with the bathwater, but after all, this is Art *History*. That does mean that dates and places are going to be of importance, though I don't say they're of supreme importance. But it helps us to understand the work if we do know something of the man's life,' said Syms, throwing his head back in an effort to bedazzle his rather unprepossessing opponent. Taking a good look at her, he surmised that it was probably sexual frustration, the curse of all fat people, that made her so antagonistic.

'That's another thing,' she went on. 'When are we going to have a little talk about why all the pictures we've been looking at are by MEN? There were plenty of female Impressionists. You've been showing us one painting after another of Parisian prostitutes. When are we going to start talking about why men like painting tarts so much, and why other men like looking at paintings of tarts? You're trying to turn something naughty and risqué and offensively sexist into something hygienic by getting all scholarly about it.'

Syms considered repeating his remark about the baby and the bathwater, but he wasn't sure of its relevance. No further comment was necessary however, because it was already well past the time to break up and repair to the cafeteria for elevenses. Disappointed and confused young things, as well as a troubled thirty-one-year-old member of the class, wandered out of the room, disconsolately trying to concentrate on the memory of the Splendid Young Man's curls, or veering off on to the question of Twix or Penguin bar with their tea.

Determined to secure the poor duck's allegiance or at least silence, Syms sidled boldly up to Pol. 'If you'd like to meet me for a drink tonight, perhaps we could discuss why men paint prostitutes,' he murmured in her ear, past the outrageous ear-ring she'd installed there.

'Trying to pick up the baby with soft soap, eh? Likely to slip out of your fingers,' Pol admonished, though she was not immune to such an approach.

Syms looked hurt. Syms definitely looked hurt. Lionel Syms was in fact easily hurt: somewhere deep inside Syms was an awareness that life could be painful and difficult. Pol felt sorry for the inner Syms.

'All right,' she said. 'Meet you at the Tunnel about eight.' (The Tunnel being a Soho bar specializing in tequila and vaginal iconoclasm.)

Pol on Men

As Pol stomped off to use the Female Staff Loo, she contemplated the gender gap. Pol knew men to be weak, cautious and coy, needing to be courted, coaxed, cossetted, and then still completely undependable. So why does society humour them? Why is it that whatever men do seems more interesting and more significant than what women do? Even gardening and cooking acquire some credibility when a man is in charge. If a woman plants some flowers, so what? If a man takes to planting irises, the whole endeavour becomes poetic. It's ART.

Why this engorged sense of their own importance? What fuels their self-love? BALLS. They're all bursting with pride in their balls their whole lives long. Men derive a boost from having balls, their enthusiasm only partially quelled by the fact that half the world has balls.

But this is why they die sooner than women. They're exhausted by the effort to keep quiet on the only subject that really interests, astounds and forever pleases them: their bat and two balls. They talk on and on around the point – like a verbal wank – skirting with varying success the central topic, that from their bodies dangles some flesh that can extend or contract more or less at will. It makes them poor company. It makes them useless about the house. This love that dare not speak its name turns men into duplicitous beings.

On this capricious contraption rests all sense of certainty. Syms was always talking about this or that artist having the BALLS to do something or other. He made it sound as if without balls, one would do nothing. As if ova and wombs were unsuggestive of creativity. And then, having claimed for balls this great significance, he dared to criticize people for not putting their balls ON THE LINE. What did this phrase mean exactly? Was it like trying to walk in a straight line when drunk? Sign on the dotted line? It surely had nothing to do with clothes-lines. Pol thought that putting a breast or an ear-lobe on the line might be equivalent. But she knew that for men, only seeing BALLS on the line would do. Men see no point in being female. There IS no point, no point like their point.

The best solution would be to deprive men of distractions from their central theme and allow them to sit around all day studying their balls. Like drone bees, they could be shelved, to be used as mere genetic stock cubes. They are experts in uselessness. Women do everything better.

Pol on Women

Pol had learned to hate women. At the least provocation
they were likely to report you to the police or the Inland
Revenue. She was sick of their scowls and scolds. They
wrapped you up in Brownie knots – moral strictures
invented at a moment's notice – and talked about you
behind your back. The trouble with crossing a woman is
you don't know you've crossed her until months or even
years later when everything pours out in some dreadful
heart-to-heart. She wasn't sure women were right that talking about a problem helps. In some ways, Pol appreciated
the obtuse silence of men on most subjects of any significance. At least you know where you are. Women fight like
cowards, always popping up out of the grass at you for
some frank talking. Preposterous people.

Pol had a feminist friend who wanted Pol to meet a man
she knew. She didn't fancy him but hoped Pol would. Pol
had duly consorted with the guy for a few weeks, and then
dropped him. The feminist friend had then ostracized Pol
on the grounds of her cruelty. But what business was it of
hers? SHE'd found the guy totally unattractive. Pol had
found him totally unattractive but briefly tolerable. Where
did morality come into it? Guilt-mongers, that was what
women were. Whatever happened to that feminist Utopia
in which women would be free to do what they wanted?

Instead the world was full of watchful women, still waiting to pounce on you if you didn't baby a man.

Pol didn't trust feminists, or anyone else who declared a political position. They were badly toilet-trained. They used politics as a nappy, in case their baser instincts got out of hand. They wanted to see their own personal madness reflected in the misshapenness of the outside world – this made them feel on top of things. They were just looking for excuses to put down huge swarms of fellow beings.

To trust anyone was madness indeed, concluded Pol, readjusting her pink and orange garb. And stomping out of the loo, she almost trampled Angelica Lotus, who had been waiting outside for ten minutes. She was fond of her loo, and would use no other.

Pol Transported

Pol, a woman without compunction and harbouring a hedonic hankering for raw fish, fumbled her way into a silver taxi and voiced her desire to be taken to the Scrimi Perturbi Sushi Bar in Covent Garden. She made the decision whether to ignore or fuck the driver (there were for her few interesting in-betweens) on the basis of the colour of his taxi. It was to ignore him.

'WHERE'd you say you were going, Miss?' asked the driver, enthralled by her, he knew not why.

A silence ensued.

''Scuse me, Miss, but I didn't quite catch –' But he did catch Pol's discouraging glare in his rear-view mirror, so he took her to the Scrimi Perturbi Sushi Bar in Covent Garden without further ado. Left in comparative peace in the back seat of the swerving vehicle, Pol squirmed out of her blue-and-green spattered tights and various other garments within reach that had been contributing to a certain over-heating problem all morning, and soon arrived at her own approximation of stylish disarray.

Chris was already engrossed in a ball of sticky rice encrusted with abalone and seaweed, with the nonchalant notion of a carrot amid a smudge of green horse-radish sauce at its apex. But he managed to acknowledge Pol's arrival by a slight but definite alteration in the alignment of his eyebrows. She plonked herself down on a stool, poured more sake into Chris's cup and drank it down.

'Order more stuff,' said Chris hospitably, when he was able. The sushi chef was soon despatched with Pol's order, which involved his chopping raw tuna, distending king prawns, coagulating rice particles and generally decimating the vegetable kingdom while a decorous, deferential, kimonoed girl bustled about with great authenticity and some ineffectuality before finally coming up with another tiny vase of sake and a cup.

Putting a hand on Chris's thigh, Pol nibbled some pale pink pickled ginger, her eyes twinkling – having suddenly felt like nibbling and twinkling. Chris stuck a spare finger into her skirt against her spine. He was enjoying the recent spate of assignations with Pol. They were meeting for lunch almost every day, sometimes skipping lunch altogether to go fuck in the loo of some pub like the Porcupine, where they'd stood straight as two quills, or the Dog and Bone, where Pol had gone down on all fours before him and he had yelled, 'Bow-wow!'

The Tunnel of Love

Lionel Syms dressed casually for his date with Pol: a volu-
minous white eighteenth-century blouse so that she would
not feel too out of proportion next to him, tight green
corduroy trousers, and a red bandanna around his fairly
athletic neck. What would the poor girl herself wear? Something black and baggy to hide the flab, he would imagine
(he hadn't taken much notice of her or her sartorial prefer-
ences up until that day). But whatever she looked like, he
would have to make an effort to give her a good time. He
did not appreciate having such a destructive element in his
seminars.

Big though she was, there was no sign of Pol in the
Tunnel, even after his eyes had adjusted to the gloom and
the degenerate crowd. The place was not quite his style, as
he knew already from previous rendezvous with female
students there. Inhabiting an abandoned stretch of the
Piccadilly Line, the Tunnel consisted of one long tubular
room. The curved walls were covered with day-glo paintings of female legs wrapped around dark geometrical
shapes. The furnishings were rough things made of wood,
there were no hors-d'oeuvres accompanying the drinks, and
the atmosphere (though Syms would have denied going
anywhere for the atmosphere) was disagreeably dissolute.
It smacked too much of underground notions for his taste.

He ordered a jug of margaritas with two glasses and sat down at a central table. He had no doubt that she would come – very few young women missed a chance to be alone with Lionel Syms. None the less, halfway through the jug, he did begin to feel stood-up, but was unable to stand up himself and depart. He was further stunned by a drum-beat which shook the floor. Or was it a person that, in time with the drums, was causing the floor to shake? He was thinking he would have preferred them to put on a Frank Sinatra record, when a red eye winked at him. There was no doubt it was winking at him, although he could find no face to go with it. On further investigation, Syms was appalled to see that the eye was completely surrounded by wiggling white flesh, and that the whole obscene and hideous invention was actually a frontal porcine portion of Pol, who danced half-naked close to his face before jiggling off to confront some other table. It was the jewel in her belly-button that had winked.

It was definitely time to go, but he couldn't move. The drum-beat rocked him as she rolled, until he longed to clutch her just to make her still. She ascended a nearby table-top and started undulating. The coital movements of her pelvis, or what he had to assume must be her pelvis, astounded him. He associated coital movements with sex, and sex with thin people. He was not used to fat people moving forwards, backwards, sideways, or in any other direction, with flamboyance. And in all this iconoclasm, he found himself wondering just where Pol's vagina might be.

That was the last thing he remembered before he suddenly registered that she was sitting at his table. 'So,' he said, somewhat at a loss. 'You wanted to discuss paintings?'

'Later,' said Pol, and kissed him.

Her kiss gave Syms sensations that were entirely new to him.

Bolts of lightning coursed through his body as they had never coursed through it before.

41

It was a rapture and an ecstasy that exceeded anything he had ever dreamt of as love.

Never in his life had he felt that he must protect and love a woman as he loved Pol: unselfishly.

With a flaming desire for her happiness which came not from his body, but from his soul.

It was so wonderful that nothing else in the world mattered except her and her lips.

As she kissed him more fiercely, violently, demandingly, he saw stars.

It was as if they were flying in the sky and the stars were twinkling in their hearts.

Syms, horrified by his gushing sentiments, hurriedly hauled himself up and hastened home.

Pol's Job

Pol had not always supplemented her grant with belly-dancing. She had only recently become proficient enough at the more complex contortions. Her first job as a student had been conducting a survey of why people travelled by tube. It only called for a few hours of her time, during peak periods.

'Why are you using the Underground today, if you don't mind my asking?'

She was amused by their defensiveness, their endless self-justifying answers. As if tube-travel required a moral basis! All she wanted to know was whether or not they were depressed during their journeys on the Underground. If so, money might be allocated for some piped music.

This fruitless enquiry gave her the idea of applying for her next job, which was choosing the music to accompany the test screen on BBC2. But there was eventually less and less screening of the test screen. She had hoped it might lead to better things, like helping with *Mainly for Pleasure* on Radio 4, or even reading out the shipping forecasts ('Portland, Plymouth, Biscay ... Faroes and S.E. Iceland ...'). But it led nowhere.

Encounters with Cragshaw

I tried to keep my encounters with Cragshaw to a minimum.

So few students took his course in *Nature Morte*, I was sometimes the only one there.

I do not like being alone in a room with a man I hardly know.

I do not even like being alone in a room with a man I do know.

Especially a man like Dr Cragshaw.

And a room that smells bad.

I felt an animosity vibrating from him, as it does from villainous characters in novels.

I also saw nothing romantic about a load of slides showing tiny areas of a painting.

It did not seem to me that Chardin appeared at his best in small details taken out of context.

I had expected something more of the Catafalque Institute, Purport Place.

After all, my life savings, along with a certain amount of my mother's competition income, were paying for this.

And I was hardly ever being allowed to see an entire painting all at once!

It was not romantic.

The room was dank.

Dr Cragshaw seemed sinister.

He never put 'This is splendid!' on my essays.

He never looked me in the eye.

He seemed to have no amorous intentions whatsoever.

But suddenly one day, when I was sitting there feeling these awkward feelings and Dr Cragshaw was showing me some slides of Chardin's earliest oblong brushstroke, I noticed something familiar.

The illusionistic painting of a relief sculpture that we were looking at reminded me of a painting my mother had won in a raffle.

Alan, my step-father, had insisted on buying up most of the 10p raffle tickets.

The draw included a bottle of Liebfraumilch and a jar of mincemeat, but Alan was only interested in the dirty old painting that had come out of somebody's grandmother's garage.

This was how Alan always won competitions.

If there was a competition offer on a box of cereal, he would buy fifty boxes.

He scoured the supermarket to find these opportunities.

He spent most of his time filling out forms and coupons, inventing slogans, and rubbing silver paint off bonanza cards with a coin.

As a result of which, the flat was now full of lounge suites, microwave ovens and knick-knacks in questionable taste.

In the end, much to Alan's surprise, it was my mother's single raffle ticket that won the hamper with the painting in it.

It was a picture of angelic children carved in white stone.

I mentioned this to Dr Cragshaw.

It was astonishingly like the Chardin painting he'd shown me.

Perhaps ours was by the Master himself!

Dr Cragshaw said it was probably by a nobody.

Everyone was doing classical relief paintings in those days, and it was not even a genre in which Chardin had been particularly proficient.

Dr Cragshaw said he was merely showing me the painting as an example of oblong, as opposed to heart-shaped, brush-strokes.

I didn't trouble him further.

But I was determined to bring the painting in so that Dr Cragshaw could look at it.

Surely he, if anyone, would be able to detect the Master's hand.

So it is not surprising that I arrived in Dr Cragshaw's rooms early the next morning, with the picture under my arm.

Dr Cragshaw was lying under a table.

At first I was worried.

I thought he might have taken a tumble.

But he said he was just looking for a lost slide.

As he seemed disinclined to get up from that unusual position, I explained the nature of my mission, and asked if I could leave the picture for him to look at later.

He said yes.

I asked him where I should put it.

He suggested that I put it under the table with him.

It was all a little strange, but I felt in no position to query his way of doing things.

From his position under the table, he probably could hardly hear me anyway.

I hurried off with the customary keen apprehension and anticipation.

My days at the Catafalque were filled with the glory of love in all its odd manifestations.

For I never knew when I would see the Splendid Young Man next!

46

Nor whose shoulders he might be encircling in a jovial manner.

There was always the tantalizing possibility that they might yet again, some day, be mine.

The Rescue of Isabella

I, Isabel, at thirty-one years of age, had reached a turning-point in my life.

I was tired of watching my mother's doomed relationship with Alan, my step-father, at each stage in its inevitable decline.

Their latest argument was about whether or not they should take a trip to Malta they'd won or sell the tickets.

They should never have married, I thought, as I listened to the dreadful arguments over Malta.

My mother wanted to go.

She seemed to have no shame at all about wearing a swimming-costume.

The thought of her sunning herself in front of Alan with hardly any clothes on appalled me.

He would have an excellent opportunity to study all her faults.

I did not know how she had the nerve.

In front of a man so much younger than herself!

Alan clearly had no desire to see my mother in a swimming-costume.

It was all very unpleasant.

They should never have married.

They were not perfectly suited.

Thus, the time was ripe.

After devoting myself to my family for thirty-one years or so, it was time for me to spread my wings.

A girl at the Catafalque had offered me a room in her flat.

She lived in a Bohemian neighbourhood near King's Cross.

I thought it sounded romantic.

I had admired her for some time, on account of the way she dealt with the tutors, especially Splutters.

I could no longer refer to him as Professor Splutters.

For, on one unfortunate day that I will never forget, he . . . ex . . . posed himself to me.

I was eating my sandwich on a bench in the Gardens of the Catafalque Institute.

The pigeons were cooing, the sun beamed, and one might have expected a harmless and delightful hour could have been passed there beneath the trees.

All at once, I heard someone calling out, 'Isabella, Isabella', in a whispery sort of voice.

Which is not the sort of name or voice I'm accustomed to hearing, but I began to realize it was directed at me, and that it came from above.

Rather in the hope of seeing God than Man, I looked up.

And there was Splutters, in a state of semi-undress.

Of course I covered my face as best I could with my sandwich and rushed inside.

I did not know who was the more embarrassed, he or I.

Although there was no sign of it – I mean of his embarrassment – during his class, which I had to attend later that day.

Afterwards, he was standing by the door like a priest, seeing people out.

Feeling fragile after our arboreal experience, I was anxious to escape quickly, but found myself delayed by his hand upon my arm.

He spoke to me of Kant.

I, who stutter over the names of philosophers.

I, who cannot pronounce 'human' for the Hume in it.

I, who falter over 'sartorial' because of Sartre.

I, who therefore had always dreaded more than anything the day when I would be required to say something about Kant.

I, who felt faint with repulsion towards Splutters and his thingy anyway.

His hand upon my arm.

His tomatoey tie.

His dishevelled appearance.

He, who had obviously reclothed himself with careless haste.

And yet I felt incapable of escaping his evil grasp.

Then Pol, a rather big sort of girl, briskly flung me through the door in front of her, and Splutters had to let go.

I was free!

Sensing my feminine helplessness and gratitude, Pol dabbed at my eyes with a tissue.

She offered to give me a few tips on how to deal with such occasions in future.

I was intrigued.

And it was thus that I met my future flat-mate.

She was not as pretty as I.

In fact she was rather overweight.

I hoped she would let me help her go on a diet.

Then I would be able to return the good deed she had done me that day.

We would both meet the men of our dreams.

The man of your dreams is worth losing weight for.

So I informed my mother that I was moving out.

She made no objection to my plan.

Alan, my step-father, told me to make the most of my salad days.

Our Heroine's New Life

Pol's flat was very untidy.

I managed to make my mark on it right away.

She was surprised when I got the Hoover out.

She hadn't realized there was one.

The only thing in the fridge was some Stolichnaya vodka, and that was in the freezer compartment.

The place needed tea and toast in a big way!

But, despite her obvious faults, Pol was well worth knowing.

She was a fund of information.

She knew how to make telephone calls without them appearing on the bill – a trick she had learned from a man.

She knew a lot about men.

Once I asked her if it hurt men to shave.

She uttered a succession of blasphemous phrases, the gist of which was that if men had kept quiet all these years about the suffering they endured whilst shaving, she would forgive them everything.

I sometimes felt that Pol was rather hard on men.

Perhaps because, being an overweight person, she hadn't had much luck with them.

Of course, I never mentioned this thought.

In fact, I never used the word 'fat' in her presence, in case it hurt her feelings.

Even when we had ham and I was trimming it, I just said I was cutting off the 'white bits'.

I was also rather worried that she might feel envious of how good I looked in jeans.

So when I started living with her, I put them away and always wore skirts.

Pol on Nuts

She had long pranced across the stunned, disapproving faces of England's modest hordes. But she had never taken one under her wing. Pol was sometimes so dumbstruck by Isabel's behaviour that she wondered if there had been a degree of insanity in her offer to Isabel of a room in her flat. But she couldn't afford to live there alone. And Isabel was fascinated by Pol, which is always pleasing.

She felt too that Isabel badly needed her help. Something had to be done about Isabel's perpetual virginity, if only because it was grating increasingly on Pol's nerves. She was prepared to deflower Isabel herself if necessary – anything to stop the woman talking and washing up for a few minutes. And Pol rather liked the way Isabel looked in jeans. She had a perfect, slightly too fulsome ass.

But guiding Isabel through all her anxieties was a daunting task. Pol's wisdom often took the form of a tirade. Isabel once complained that people seemed to treat her differently when they found out she was allergic to nuts.

'OK, so you're allergic to nuts!' yelled Pol, attempting to be pleasant about it but failing. 'You don't beat people up or steal their pension books, you don't rape and pillage. You're just a little awkward about curries and cakes. You're no good to anyone who likes experimenting with foreign confectionery, this is true. Nuts make you itch. I admit it makes you a lousy dinner guest. But there are people in this world who object to women who wear red lipstick! Compared to that, what's a little aversion to brazil nuts?'

Isabel was comforted by this, despite the abrasive tone. In fact, Pol's headstrong manner often reminded Isabel of the romantic heroines in Babs Cartwheel's novels.

One Summer Evening

The outing was not a success. It had taken place in Brent-
ford. Pol met Chris there for a fourth-century Greek play,
made into a musical and staged in a swimming-pool. The
props consisted of a great many inflatable toys of every
variety. The weather was warm, there was no ventilation in
the viewing area above the pool, and the entire audience
was fainting from the heat. Pol's feet had swollen inside her
shoe-fetishist high-heels, and trains back to civilization were
infrequent.

She and Chris had not found it an erotically inspiring
experience, and they parted glumly at Waterloo in search
of different night buses. But by this time, Pol could hardly
walk. She hailed a cab: it was to be one of those extremely
expensive pleasureless evenings. Perhaps she was tiring of
Chris. His conventional home-life and unoriginal though
ardent adultery depressed her. She saw it reflected in all
the dingy flats she glimpsed through uncurtained windows
as she sped home. By the time she arrived, she was lost in
ill-humoured reverie. Another sore point was that just ahead
of them as they neared her place was the night bus she
should have caught.

'That'll be £3.20,' said the taxi-driver.

Pol gave him a five-pound note and, being a good tipper,
said, 'Just give me one.'

'Just GIVE you one?' he smirked lasciviously. 'I'd like to give YOU one any time, love.'

Pol laughed. She was pleased with his emphasis. She was taken with his dirty inflections and his keen eyes. 'Perhaps you'd like to come in for a moment and we could discuss the matter,' she said.

They managed to get inside the door and get the door shut and get more or less beyond the unerotic straw mat (Isabel's only contribution to the flat so far) before his hands were gripping her ass and her legs encircled his. Their moans were in miniature, through haste and secrecy. They both wanted it fast. No desire for courtship or condoms. He seemed so big. SHE seemed so big. Two strangers with a shared sense of scale.

Isabel slept right through this, but she was to become aware of the taxi-driver on a few subsequent occasions. It mystified her that, wherever Pol's men came from, they always came back. They clamoured, they clambered, for attention, and Pol had to deal severely with them. She had no time for mere repetitions of delicious events.

The 32-year-old Woman Walks Home

I decided to walk back to Pol's place that day.

It wasn't far to King's Cross.

Especially when one is in love.

I wondered if he felt the chemistry between us.

The way I melted when he arrived in the cafeteria.

His tray next to mine as we searched for something edible.

It was tantalizing.

It was cruel.

It was delightful.

It was unbearable.

He was so tall, athletic and aristocratic.

He was young and splendid, and he liked me!

I was sure of it.

On my way home, I noticed a book-shop on a corner.

Perhaps they would have one of the Splendid Young Man's books on Impressionism.

If it was in paperback, I would definitely buy it.

I felt it was time I read the Splendid Young Man's books.

I had enjoyed many exciting afternoons looking for them on the shelves of the Catafalque library, but had never found any.

When I entered the shop, I was pleased to discover that it specialized in art books.

I did not dare ask for assistance in my quest.

I feared I might blush inordinately.

And not at all becomingly.

Like some sort of freak, really.

Yet the shop-keeper already seemed to be looking at me as if I were a little surprising.

I took this to be because I'm a somewhat old-fashioned dresser.

I turned shyly to further peruse the books.

But the shop-keeper interrupted my tantalizing investigation by asking, 'May I help you?', in a rather rough way.

He had an American accent.

I immediately took against him.

What business do Americans have selling books on Art History in the middle of London?

Books probably by beautiful Englishmen!

Is nothing sacred?

To hide my indignation, I pretended I hadn't heard the little man.

I could tell he was little, even though he was sitting behind a desk.

Women know these things.

Then he said, 'Can I help you, please?'

This time more insistently, more demandingly, more impatiently.

More manfully, if you like.

'Thank you,' I replied coolly. 'I'm just browsing.'

I think one should be allowed to wander around a book-shop at one's own leisurely pace.

I do not like being hurried.

I, who have never been allowed to discover my own natural speed.

I . . .

He spoke again!

This time he said, 'Yes, but you see, Madam, this is not a

book-store. This is my flat. You are standing in my study, casting an eye over my books, when I have not in fact invited you in, which would have been unlikely since I do not know you, and what's more, I am trying to read.'

This stunned me rather.

'I know, I know,' he went on. 'The window looks like a shop window. That is because this used to be a shop. But now it is not a shop.'

The door was still ajar, I was relieved to observe.

Having thought I was entering a bona fide book-shop, here I was, alone with a strange man in his study!

Who was gazing at me piercingly.

He had a striking air of determination about him.

And quite a manly physique in some ways.

There was a cynical twist to his lips.

His hair was very short.

It would no doubt have been curly, had he allowed it to grow long enough to bend.

His rough-shaven chin suggested to me animal passion.

There was not enough time to make a thorough investigation of his physiognomy.

It was however quite clear to me that he was not my Mr Right.

He was not tall, dark and handsome.

He was one or two of these things, but not all three at once.

Of course I was willing to make exceptions, as I had already done in the case of Lionel Syms's blond curls.

This man was at least not blond.

But he was very rude.

And pretending to be a shop-keeper in order to lure unsuspecting young women into his study suggested to me that he was daring, deceitful and dangerous.

So I said with what spirit I could summon in such a compromising situation, 'Well! If everything here is YOURS, I will be going.'

And I went.

Afterwards, I felt totally flustered, as is usual with me after a romantic encounter with a man.

Even if it is with an American one.

Even if it is with a rude American one.

(Though strangely attractive.)

Despite my flustered state, I had the presence of mind to estimate the chances of our ever meeting again.

In the novels of Babs Cartwheel, a reunion would have been inevitable.

But the world is very crowded these days.

And I didn't move in many circles.

Except those of my own making.

I reckoned there was about a 2% chance.

Our Hero at Last

His had been a normal fifties American plaid pyjamas child-hood. He had been kept occupied by hamsters, electric train sets (in which the hamsters were forced to travel), Boy Scout meetings, mountain-climbing, bike-hikes and TV. His sister had sexually molested him, tickling his penis in a way they both enjoyed until she got bored and turned to Barbie dolls. She later ended up running a gas station in Wyoming, with which she was also bored. She always seemed to him somewhat adrift.

His mother was ill and clingy. She would welcome him into her arms and her darkened bedroom when he got home from the day's bullying at school. She smelled of baby powder and cod liver oil. He did too, probably. Together they would eat Frito's Corn Chips, which he hated, and watch whatever TV programme they could reach agreement on. As there were fewer shows a grown-up would tolerate, he compromised more on this than she did.

His father drove a big car. He drove it off in the morning and eventually drove it back. Sometimes his returns were made more noteworthy by his acquisition of Chinese food or pizza on the way home. When he wasn't too tired, he and his son would go outside and play ball, which consisted of throwing the ball too hard or too high for the boy to catch it. Immensely satisfying to watch one's son scrambling in a bush for a ball. If the boy threw a fast one, his father went indoors.

The boy preferred to go inside too and watch his sister baking green cake (for St Patrick's Day) or knitting wool jewellery. But she never played with his balls again. He became a solitary type who practised magic tricks for hours in front of the mirror in his bedroom that was hung too high for him, so that he had to do the tricks at shoulder, even chin, level.

He mastered 'The Ghostly Pencil', 'Vapour of the Yogi', 'The Melting Coin', 'Solid Water', 'The Obedient Orange', 'The Lazy Match', 'Phantom Smoke', 'Floating Sugar Cubes', 'The Mystery Banana' and some simplified Houdini escapes. He hoped to amaze and perplex his family. But his sister had a habit of indifference to him. His mother was imperturbable with damp cotton wool pads over her eyes, sunk in gloom and oil. His father was nowhere. Standing sturdily in front of a mirror in the half-light of afternoon in the dark ages of fifties America, he practised his tricks.

This was how he got his accent, his sense of humour, his sweetness, his stiffness, his uncertainty, his hypochondria, his bad eyes, his fear of women, and his collection of kitsch memorabilia. Which wasn't really a collection, until he realized there was too much to throw away, and that it had become kitsch.

Well, what was he supposed to do with himself for his first twenty years? Make a million, fly to the moon, grow asparagus?

Our Hero's Mother

For many years she thought she was dying. Her life was a series of anti-climaxes, leading up to that final anti-climax. She lay around listening to the sound of tea-bags brewing in the tea-pot in the hallway. She could not bear to be too close to the tea at this stage. Even through the wall she could hear the molecules in the tea giving up hope of staying as they had been, so stagnant and at ease in their dry state. She heard them surrender themselves to their hot, their liquid fate, she listened to their noiseless acceptance of this completely unforeseen development.

The highlight of her life was menstruation. She felt her body building up to this event. It held her in suspense, since she was never sure when the storm was due to break. Her breasts got sore, days, sometimes ten days, before. She liked the explosion of blood that finally came to punctuate her life.

But menstruation didn't want to be loved, and took its revenge. Once, when she stood up in a room full of her husband's poker pals, there on the chair behind her and on the back of her flowery dress was the evidence of her exciting double life, the activity so far removed from male games. The dress was not the problem. That could be dealt with by backing out of the room. But the chair? Yes, she took the chair out with her as well.

Our Hero's Mother Again

Her first child had been run-of-the-mill, an essential accoutrement among her friends who had all married to have children and had children in order to feel married.

She'd gone through the baby shower routine, smiling insincerely at each new baby item in pink, white and sky-blue, a pale imitation of the colours of the American flag and geared for a baby of any description. She had worn all the hand-me-down maternity dresses, their tattered frills half-mended by harassed mothers. She'd shown the requisite delight in her bulging belly at the grocery store, while looking for cigarettes and anything else that might cheer her up. She had endured the humiliation of no longer fitting into the swivel seat at the hair salon and having to sit with the old ladies. She'd fallen tumultuously in and out of love with her obstetrician.

She'd been through all the pooh-poohed and prettified embarrassments of pregnancy, followed by the unimagined indignities of giving birth. And then the struggle to breast-feed, doomed and distrusted from the start. She was better at preparing the wrist-hot bottles of formula, a precise science performed under trying conditions, for the kid was always crying and her breasts too wept and ached to do their duty.

She felt that only a baby could get away with such

prolonged persecution of a law-abiding citizen without being locked up. The whining, the vomiting, the crying, the diarrhoea, the rashes, the whining. The sleepless plod to the crib while trying to get her murderous impulses under control. A thing barely human that had to be served with superhuman devotion and struggle. People are not less troublesome according to size.

She had a diaper service at least. A man came to the door to collect the dirty diapers from which the shit had been carefully scraped. He delivered a bunch of clean ones, on which the shit was instantly deposited.

There was all the boredom of being at home so much – not since her own infancy had she been so housebound and friendless. She didn't want to see her friends, in case they noticed the blankness in her. Of course, in the end there was all the thankless socializing involved in PTA meetings, Xmas plays, Brownie outings, swimming lessons, piano lessons, ice-skating and Hallowe'en: she dressed the kid as a blob, a devil, a cigarette box.

But when the second one emerged rather effortlessly from her womb, she changed. She hadn't noticed with the first how beautiful a baby's eyelids are. She'd fended the child off as if she was trying to get something sticky off her fingers. But this time she didn't want to let go. She left her husband's bed to sleep with him, her son, who seemed the only thing in the world that was hers. She willingly fed him from her body, happy to encircle him, happiest when encircling him, infusing him with mother-love to make him grow.

She napped when he napped, woke when he woke, wept and laughed with him. She took him to the grocery store and was amazed to see people twisting his little fingers around theirs, as if he were just another baby in a baby boom. And then they dared to change the subject and ask, 'And how does Sandy like having a little brother?' 'How IS Sandy?' 'WHERE is Sandy?'

Sandy was at school. Sandy was usually at school. And her mother felt these questions as an affront. Why was she not allowed to love her son? People gave her no peace about it. They were determined to recall her from her ecstasy. They did not approve of this sudden acquisition of maternal feelings. Even her own mother seemed increasingly stern over the phone. She no longer wanted to inform her mother of the latest indications of the baby's perfections.

But finally it was her mother who broke the spell, the dream-state in which she'd kept him so safe, in which she herself had felt so safe. Her mother said, 'You have GOT to give that child a name.' As if she was Queen Victoria or something. As if she was GOD or something: 'Give that child a NAME.'

So the Child was given a Name. And the intimacy between the mother and the infant who had escaped her body without pain, except that of eternal vigilance, who had been worth any ordeal anyway because he was her cushion to lie on and plump up for the rest of her life, her lonely life, the child she had called Bumple and Baba in the interim, was lost for ever. This minuscule, pre-verbal, prehensile US citizen deserved respect. No longer the outlandish sense of responsibility that made her want to keep the globe from spinning in case it dizzied him, the possessive pride in having created something that just needed a little rounding off, all the easy work still to be done, and glory assured.

She called him Robert, the name of a grown man who has already left home. Only echoes, half-remembered gestures of their love-affair remained. It was the beginning of the end.

Our Hero's Education

She taught him at home for as long as she could. She eagerly set about making him the man that everyone wanted, a man who would escape her grasp. She taught him to do household chores, so that as she dusted, he followed along below with a small broom. She sang him opera highlights at the piano, freely translating from languages she didn't know and inventing her own outrageous plots. She taught him the essential thing in life: how to play solitary card games. And she worried about when it would be necessary to inform him of death. One of these days a doctor would tell her she had months to live, she moved forever in a cloud of decay, she could smell it all around her. How to explain to a child that he and you will some day die? That you brought him into a world in which such unbearable things are to be borne, and that you yourself have long understood and accepted that you and he will some day die? Every aspect of awareness, whittled down and rounded off, cultivated and captivated by life, to be dented, denied and finally destroyed by death. In every beginning its end. This was not dinner-table conversation!

'When we made you, a bit of your Daddy and a bit of me went into you,' she told him one day. 'And that's why you look a bit like him and a bit like me, and even behave a bit like us.'

'I guess that's why you made me a bit peculiar.'

It was time he went to school.

The night before Robert started kindergarten, his mother dreamt she found him hanging naked from the bath-tub shower tap. He had committed suicide because she was sending him to school. His body was cold. But when she loosened the string around his neck, he stirred. He was saved! She held him close, caressing the small, helpless head, weeping and crooning over him, 'Baba, my Baba.'

'Don't call me Baba,' he said, reviving.

The next morning, she took him to school with some trepidation. She feared he would never forgive her. Her dream baby would feel betrayed. But the living actual boy was eager to go to school. He wanted to catch up with his sister, Sandy.

The teacher's name was Miss Roberts. She said it must be fate that Robert was in her class. This was an unfortunate word under the circumstances, too close to 'fatal'. Robert's mother didn't feel encouraged by it, under the circumstances. Under the circumstances, she longed to get home so that she could collapse. She watched him line up limply behind his class and plod into the low building as if it were the gas chamber.

But Robert loved school. They had tadpoles there, and a large marble-run with ramps and jumps and bridges and slots and tunnels for large blue marbles. He developed crushes on little girls, whom he tried to sleep next to at nap-time, when they all lay down flat on the floor. And he was urged to believe all manner of unlikely but gratifying things about the United States of America and its place in the universe.

'There are two kinds of roots,' he told his mother. 'Tap roots and bushy roots.'

'Oh?'

'And some plants eat each other. And some eat animals.'

'Oh, like the Venus Fly Trap!' yelled Sandy.

'Yes,' Robert said, annoyed. 'The Venus Fly Trap. That eats bugs. Some plants drink tea.'

'Are you sure?' asked his mother.

'Yeah, my teacher gives her roses tea to drink.'

His mother grimly acknowledged that she had been supplanted by this woman who couldn't possibly appreciate the miracle of Robert's legs and arms, his nose that was still a baby's nose, a woman who didn't know his favourite foods and probably didn't care. Who surely didn't realize the sweetness of him. A woman who would never have noticed him hanging in the shower.

But school had its compensations. At Thanksgiving he brought home a picture of a turkey, made in the shape of his own hand, and on the back it said, 'Mommy I love you.'

Our Hero's Hamsters

He practised serial monogamy with his hamsters: one at a time. The first was called Amelia. She never bit. Towser was another favourite, valiant Towser, who'd seemed the most at ease when riding in the cattle-car of the electric train, in and out under Robert's bed. But none of them was exactly happy.

Our Hero's Sister Sandy

Sandy drank a lot of Coke. She liked the harshness of it in her throat – it must be the bubbles exploding, she thought. She often pondered the problems of molecules. She felt that too much movement, for instance, was hard on the human body. This is why it's tiring to travel. The molecules have to exert themselves to hold the whole construction together when the body is in motion. This is also why vacuum cleaners can never be liked. Vacuum cleaners cause a great deal of molecular uproar.

Robert never realized his friendship with Sandy had a beginning, a middle and an end. He forgot it had begun. He never knew that his mother, peeping through a crack in the door one day when a suspicious silence had filled the house, saw Sandy squeezing his penis. Sandy was yanked out into the backyard and slapped.

'You don't do that to my son, you little bitch!' Words Sandy had never heard before sprang from her mother's mouth. Octopus arms entangled her.

Sandy never touched Robert again without uneasiness, even repulsion. She never touched any man without fear of hidden consequences. A crucial element of parental permission was never granted. Her mother seemed to find sex distasteful and never spoke of it. She never even explained to Sandy the rudiments of menstruation. In the end, all was revealed when a friend noticed Sandy's red-stained skirt after gym, and helped her to wash it and then the bench Sandy had been sitting on.

Her father died without telling her he loved her. He had not even managed to teach her how to use a cheque-book. He died without telling her her Social Security Number. It was only boredom that calmed Sandy's soul, and a recurrent sexual fantasy which involved cats eating mice, naughty bits first.

Our Hero's Adolescence

After the death of his father, who was not much mourned except by Sandy, Robert had most of the responsibility of taking care of his mother. She was not to be outdone by her husband, and proceeded to come down with a succession of serious illnesses. Dragged in to visit her after her mastectomy, the boy was appalled by an orangey-pink liquid draining from the hidden wound into a plastic bag. The doctors called it serum, but Robert thought they were saying 'syrup'. He was disgusted by the thought of putting that on his pancakes.

She had skin cancer on one eyelid, the treatment for which was to place a metal plate over the eye-ball and then zap the eyelid with radiation, entirely without anaesthetic. It usually took legions of incompetent nurses to get the metal plate on to the eye, while Robert held his mother's hand. And this agony was inflicted three times a week for a month.

They operated on her brain once. In Intensive Care he met her shaved head and her pale moon face. Another moon to stare at him without knowing him. She fingered the patterned holes in the hospital blanket, with no idea that it was a hospital or a blanket. He gave the moon creature a ring, which she fingered in her childish way. But she seemed to like it. He put it on her finger. When she was better, not knowing how she had acquired it, she threw the cheap thing away.

Robert had no opportunity to be a difficult teenager, but he did fall in love. Gail seduced him. She took him to the movies. They smoked grass on the beach and kissed among sand dunes. Robert considered himself the first person to see a correlation between breasts and sand dunes. Gail's pubic triangle was another lesson in geometry. In return, he showed Gail his magic tricks, that he'd practised so assiduously all alone. 'Contrary to public belief, you don't have to have large hands to palm a card.'

His mother shrieked at him for going out so much when she was ill. But he had his own bones of contention. She was ALWAYS ill. Where had she been all his life? In bed or on the couch. His friends annoyed their parents by not turning up on time for dinner. HE had to COOK the dinner.

And Gail loved him. The ancient baby in him needed that. The baby in him remembered a prehistoric, prehensile time when a woman had wrapped him up in her love. The loss of which was something he'd hoped to amend ever since – with magic tricks if necessary.

Our Hero's Job

Escaping to Yale, Robert was still inundated with his mother's needs, transmitted by letter. Her every headache was recorded and sent off by air mail.

He was pleased to be offered a Junior Lectureship at the Catafalque in London while still a graduate student. Academic jobs were scarce and an additional 3,000 miles between him and his mother had its appeal. He immediately set about selling off the kitsch paraphernalia with which he was still encumbered, to finance his trip. The Mickey Mouse lamp-shade had to go – a collector's item, it fetched $300. The lamp-stand had been made from an ancient Milk of Magnesia bottle – $45. The walls of his graduate apartment on St Ronan Street, in a rather beautiful part of New Haven, were covered with fifties ads and movie posters – $200 each. And so it went. Bottle tops, baseball cards, old hairspray cans, his pink poodle place-mats, his plastic DNA molecule, his Leopold Stokowski cigarette-lighter/ash-tray, the lot.

So it was somewhat to his dismay that he found on arrival in London that he did not have a job at the Catafalque Institute after all. A man named Lionel Syms had got it. In all his arrangements for his move to England, Robert had forgotten to sign the contract the Catafalque had sent him. He'd thought it was just a formality. The arrival of

Robert in person would be proof enough of his acceptance of the post. But Lionel Syms (then a mere part-time sycophant at the Catafalque), among others (those particularly subject to anti-American sentiments), chose to believe that Robert didn't want the job after all. It must be admitted that the academic climate in Britain in the early eighties did not encourage gracious acceptance of defeat: Syms was aware that if he failed to get a lectureship at the Catafalque at this stage, he would be stuck for many years in some provincial backwater awaiting the death of Splutters, Cragshaw, Basilisk or the rest, with every chance that even then, given the cuts in educational spending by the government, there would be no vacancies. Desperate times.

Syms tried to make it up to Robert though, by getting him various reviewing jobs on low-budget magazines like *Time Out*. Robert wrote for *The Times Literary Supplement* too, for the sake of its American circulation. He was busily applying for jobs back home now.

But he lingered. There was something about the quiet anonymity of London that agreed with him. He liked pubs. They were less depressing than bars in America, which were kept puritanically dingy. One could drink an indecent amount in a pub and still feel civilized. And through Syms, whom he occasionally met for a drink, he'd found a great flat. He gained weight, made friends, wrote to his mother, and stayed put, except for two weeks at home every Christmas.

Suffering a little from the stodgy cuisine of his adopted country, he opened the front door one day to let in a little air. Instead, in waltzed Isabel, an odd figure in her long skirt and high heels. He noted that her hair was brown and her eyes translucent blue.

The Splendid Young Man's Proposal

The Catafalque Institute was not holding up well in the modern world in one particularly pressing respect: its finances were in terrible shape. None of its directors had ever been any good at mathematics; they even went so far as to be proud of this disability. But now something had to be done. Of the many members of staff whose services were no longer required, none had volunteered for redundancy. That they might have out-stayed their welcome was of no matter. The essential absurdity of the Catafalque was founded on the fact that here the untenable was taught by the tenacious. The Catafalque boasted a great number of insensible people professing sensibility, undaunted by the most awkward rational impulse. Catalfalquians were not voluntary redundancy material.

Accepting more foreign students had been contemplated, as these were forced to pay huge fees. But who wanted a load of foreigners trotting about the place? It was also understood that the Institute's minor collection of paintings could reach high prices at Sotheby's if the market was handled properly, but the Catafalque had never sunk to selling its collection, and the novelty of the idea was not in its favour.

Meanwhile, the outlay of resources was becoming a nuisance. There was the aged lift to consider. It had to be kept in good order to keep the aged staff going up and down. The marbled pillars needed retouching. In fact, it had even been suggested that the grand but crumbling structure in Purport Place should be abandoned to property developers, and new premises sought in Woolwich or Willesden.

Intent on avoiding such a catastrophe, the Finance Committee called a general meeting, to see if they could ransack the tutors' minds for an inspiring idea. The response was not, on the whole, helpful. Some individuals were actually prepared to joke about the matter. Sir Humphrey wittily offered to have a word with the Palace about it. Perhaps the Queen would organize a Jumble Sale for them. Dr Lotus said quite seriously that she would be happy to devote her spare hours to writing a best-selling novel, if that would be of any assistance. Splutters said he was keen to do some extra private tutoring. Cragshaw said not a word, worried mainly that he might be forced to cut back on camera film.

Only the Splendid Young Man, spurred on by personal antipathy, managed to come up with a scheme which stirred the imagination. After an initial sounding-out of support, he prepared a short paper which he tacked up on the Staff Room bulletin board a few days later.

The Splendid Young Man's Actual Written Proposal

Sirs,

The history of our Gardens, despite their prime position behind Purport Place, is one of declining use. How are we to account for this, when any student is welcome, if weather allows, to roam the verdant paths and mossy beds? No doubt it is not my place here to make assertions regarding a certain member, as it were, of staff, who can sometimes be sighted therein, pursuing activities of varying appropriateness considering the high aims of this institution. I refer of course to particular uses of the umbrella, unrelated to rain.

There is also the eyesore at the bottom of the Gardens, a prefab, where I believe an obscure scholarly endeavour is being conducted. I'm sure most of you will agree that what the Gardens need is a wholesome new image.

It is my humble belief that this could be effected through the introduction of a good all-weather tennis court. Even Art Historians need to keep trim! I myself take exercise of some sort every day. With the advent of a tennis court, not only would the Catafalque be able to hold its own against the charms of other colleges offering leisure facilities, but the aforementioned activities might be tactfully discouraged. The Gardens might then be more at the disposal of those students and tutors who are able to maintain a decent level of decorum. An increased intake of students, combined with the sad but inevitable decline in the number of lecturers, would lead to great improvements in the Catafalque's finances.

I have investigated the technical details involved in my proposal, and find the most reasonable price to be in the region of £17,000. The surface would be of sand-filled artificial grass laid on a 35 mm base of bitmac above 150 mm of crushed rock bottoming. There would be a green plastic-coated chainlink perimeter fence 2.76 metres high, the dimensions being 112 × 54 feet.

If the straight lines of the court and its perimeter fence are considered aesthetically displeasing, they might easily be softened by growing a hedge, or by covering the fence with clematis, roses, honeysuckle and other creepers. I have no views on this.

The Splendid Young Man and His Tennis Court

In between the essays, full of innuendo, of students he had whipped up to a fearsome degree of admiration, and feeling sick with love for Pol (he knew not why), the Splendid Young Man energetically propounded in every quarter the beauties of his tennis court plan. The students were most enthusiastic.

An evening meeting was arranged for tutors to discuss the matter. Wine would be served. None the less, Cragshaw did not even turn up. He could see that the whole business was a subtle attempt to drive him out, thus freeing his prefab for tennis rackets and *après-sport* trysts. He was particularly irked by Syms's attempt, in his elaborations on the subject of gravel and perimeter fencing and such things, to imitate, perhaps even to outdo, Cragshaw's own aptitude for practical information.

But those who did attend the meeting had many interesting questions to put to the Splendid Young Man, not least because this prolonged the rare opportunity to drink wine at the Catafalque's expense. Sir Humphrey gallantly got the ball rolling.

'If it is merely the students we wish to please, would not a fairground roller-coaster or an all-night bar attract as many to our noble halls, Lionel, and even bring in some revenue of their own, which I take it the tennis court will not do?'

'No, we will certainly not be asking people to pay for use of the court,' replied Syms. 'That would not be in keeping with the impression of gentlemanly ease we would wish to create. Nor would a roller-coaster, though very wittily suggested, Sir Humphrey.'

'Would there be some noise involved?' asked Angelica Lotus, who now planned to write a novel anyway, along with various other plans she was hatching.

'For myself, I find the sound of tennis pleasantly evocative. However, with so many trees, it would not carry far,' said Syms, returning every volley with becoming restraint.

'I object on aesthetic grounds,' spluttered Splutters.

'Our perception of what is ugly depends largely on the context,' murmured Syms, thinking of Pol.

'There is a distinction,' Splutters blustered on, 'between formal gardens, ornamental gardens, parkland gardens, woodland gardens and gardens full of tennis balls, would you not agree?'

'I was not aware of your great respect for gardens, Splutters. But to my mind, they are there to be used.'

'But a tennis court would compromise the essential integrity of the original Georgian plan,' said Splutters.

'My guess,' guessed the Splendid Young Man, 'since we ARE just guessing here, is that the original planners would not be at all surprised and would indeed welcome a tennis court.'

'Be that as it may, it is surely of limited appeal to the tutors,' pursued Splutters, losing ground.

'Actually, I have been gratified that a number of very elderly tutors have told me they look forward to coming into the Gardens after their retirement specifically to watch a game.'

'Croquet or boules would be more suitable.'

'I don't think they can have quite the same appeal or impact as tennis on a good all-weather court.'

'Well, as to weather, do you seriously believe that anyone is going to want to play tennis in the rain?'

'You could always offer them your brolly, Splutters,' sneered the Splendid Young Man.

People burped and slurped up the remains of their wine in the uncomfortable silence that followed, and after a vote, which tended shakily towards the affirmative, the gathering broke up. The Splendid Young Man, well satisfied with his proposal's progress for the time being, headed off into the darkness and dankness of London to meet Pol. He wanted to check what was in her navel tonight. He loved all her knobs and buttons, her levers and spring-catches. He was intrigued by the technicalities involved in screwing her.

Pol's Plan

By this time, Pol was finding life with Isabel almost unbearable. She considered Isabel's presence strangely corrupting. Hundreds of Babs Cartwheel books now lay on Pol's sagging shelves. They were taking over the flat. Frightening to think that Isabel's head was stuffed to the brim with these pathetically lustful, reprehensibly idealized notions. It was like living with a volcano.

What's more, Isabel was always holding her legs together. Whatever position she adopted, whether lying on the sofa watching TV or sitting in a seminar, probably even when she was getting out of a BATH-TUB, the legs were stuck firmly together. Pol had narrowed the whole problem with Isabel down to these legs. If only they were touching each other in some clandestine form of masturbation, or if Isabel had a congenital hip problem, Pol could have forgiven it.

Pol decided to seduce Isabel herself. It seemed almost a duty. She bought gin, having noticed Isabel's predilection for the stuff. They sat up late one night drinking gin and tonics, which Isabel prepared with exasperating accuracy, using a tiny measuring cup. Pol left the choice of music up to Isabel too. It was Frank Sinatra. This was to be Isabel's night, everything geared towards her satisfaction.

As usual, the conversation turned to Isabel's current fantasy objects: a few dead film stars, some still extant

TV personalities, and the Splendid Young Man at the Catafalque. Pol was supposed to help her estimate the likeliness of any of these falling passionately in love with Isabel in the foreseeable future. The two of them had long since given up discussing Pol's love-life. For Isabel it distressingly failed to strike a note of true romance. It seemed extremely shabby when seen against the bright fantasies of married life that Isabel entertained most of the day and night. No comparison, really.

'I just can't tell whether the Splendid Young Man likes me or not,' Isabel rambled dizzily on.

'Are you sure you'd like HIM if he decided he liked you?'

'Oh, he's such a fine man . . .'

'Fine men should be seen and not heard, shaken not stirred,' declaimed Pol. She was tired of his name-dropping, and his effete belief in the superiority of art over life. Pol preferred a real tree to a Constable any day. The Splendid Young Man was all balls. 'It would be a lot easier if we just liked women, don't you think?' Pol said, omitting the fact that her female paramours were just as difficult as the men, especially when abandoned.

'WHAT? Oh, I could never do that! Could you ever?'

'Ever what?' Pol poured some more gin straight from the bottle into their glasses.

'Well . . . Sleep . . . with . . . a . . . woman,' said Isabel, punctuating herself in the manner of a romantic heroine.

'Sure.'

'WHAT? Have you . . . ever . . .?'

'What's the big difference? An orgasm's an orgasm,' said Pol, doing a somersault on the floor which startlingly revealed her omission of knickers that day.

'WHAT? But surely it's . . . it's the alien . . . quality of a man that makes him . . . interesting?' said Isabel, gulping some gin and looking away.

85

'Would you stop prefacing your every stunned response with the word, "WHAT"?' said Pol, becoming dismally aware that she was losing this battle. 'Women are pretty alien too, you know, when you start thinking of them as sexual objects. In fact, that's how I think of YOU sometimes.' Resuming her place on the sofa, Pol prepared to separate those legs.

'What?' said Isabel.

'It would be very convenient, living and sleeping together. We'd save some money on the gas fires.' Pol leaned forward slowly, and gently pushed her tongue into Isabel's alien mouth and put her hand on one tiny alien breast.

After a moment of complete immobility, Isabel gasped, speechless for once, and ran to her room, locking the door. Frank Sinatra petered out. It was not one of Pol's most successful exploits.

The 32-year-old Woman's Inviolable Heterosexuality

Surprising though it may seem, I was greatly enjoying my meetings with Dr Cragshaw.

He seemed quite keen on me after all.

Or at least appreciative of my work.

Perhaps not so keen on ME.

Not in a romantic sense.

But I was not concerned about romance.

In fact, due to certain disturbing events, I was less concerned about it than usual.

For, very late one night, it had become clear that my flat-mate was IN LOVE with me.

I had always intended to help Pol with her love-life, but not in THAT way!

It was very embarrassing.

But I knew that, with time, she would probably get over it.

Meanwhile, I was thankful for the fact that she was out a lot.

I was left in peace to ill-attend myself.

I went into something of a decline.

I wore my dressing-gown all day, and buried myself in my work.

In the evenings, I watched TV and drank gin and tonics.

I felt more disgusted with myself than usual, and dealt with my bodily functions in carefully timed stints.

I planned all such embarrassments in advance and avoided them if possible.

As always when down-hearted, I said to myself that my work was the only thing that mattered.

Art History is romantic enough in itself.

And I had to prepare for my lecture engagement.

Dr Cragshaw had arranged for me to give a talk to the Workers' Educational Association in Lewes.

It was the sort of thing tutors did at the Catafalque for favoured students.

It was nothing grand, but for someone without as yet an actual degree in Art History, it was quite an honour.

This had warmed me to Dr Cragshaw.

It made up for his not having yet looked at that picture of my mother's.

Neither of us had actually mentioned the picture for over a year.

But I simply attributed this to his rather formal manner.

During my preparations for my lecture in Lewes, I began to develop a theory based on Dr Cragshaw's enlarged details of brushstrokes.

I discovered that the delicacy of Chardin's still lifes was counteracted by the Master's strong, wild and passionate handling of the paint.

There was a definite contrast between the density of the paint and the transitory illusion it created.

Lightness and heaviness, the rough and the smooth.

The forceful, the penetrating; the pliant, the receptive.

It was clearly the male and female principles in action.

All of heterosexuality was embodied there.

Of course I was too embarrassed to expound my theory to Dr Cragshaw, who would only have said it was nonsense.

But I had found the subject for my lecture.

Bad Eyesight

El Greco had bad eyes.

That's why he elongated the forms in his paintings.

That was how he saw things.

This I found out by going to a momentous evening lecture at the Catafalque, given by a guest speaker.

It was momentous not only because of El Greco, however.

It was momentous because the guest speaker was none other than the man I'd once met in peculiar circumstances, having mistaken his flat for a book-shop.

He stood manfully at the podium.

It made him look authoritative.

It made him look commanding.

Demanding.

It made him look less American.

It made him look aristocratic.

Also, his accent was softened by the acoustics of the room.

Or perhaps it had been softened by time.

Perhaps I too had been softened by time, I thought.

His name was Robert.

A name to conjure with.

A name that matched his stiff bearing.

He moved tentatively, as if he had been tied up with invisible thread.

Like a perplexed Houdini.

He looked like he needed a mother's love.

His stiffness gave him a stillness which I found very attractive.

After the talk, Pol insisted on going up to meet him.

She had no idea I had already done so.

She just wanted a drink and waddled up to the most eligible companion in the room.

And took me trailing behind her.

It was all part of her lessons for me in How To Live.

I was so embarrassed, I could have died.

I hoped he wouldn't recognize me.

When we got to the pub, he volunteered to get the drinks.

But Pol insisted on buying them, saying that he must be tired after his lecture.

Well, then I knew something was up.

Pol was usually happy for somebody else to buy the drinks.

While she was away from the table, an intriguing thing happened.

He looked at me quizzically and asked, 'Haven't we met?' and then laughed.

I couldn't think of anything to say.

For, in that split second between his quizzical look and his laugh, I had fallen madly in love.

I transferred all my allegiances, or the bulk of them at any rate, from the Splendid Young Man to Robert in a matter of moments.

It was momentous.

One of the advantages of unrequited passions, I find, is that there is no need to worry about infidelity.

One can fall in love with a new person every day and hurt no one except oneself.

No recriminations, no sulking, no painful divorce.

I was an old hand.

I was always getting crushes and getting crushed.

If only Robert and I had met sooner, I could have been spared all that.

For I knew he was The Man for me.

Everything seemed right about him.

I even altered some of my original criteria to accommodate him.

He was not tall, dark and handsome.

He was sometimes one or two of these things, but not all three at once.

I hoped in return that he would make allowances for my physical defects.

We were getting along rather well actually, until Pol came back.

She started talking about El Greco and some mad times she'd had in Toledo, bull-fights and toreadors and I don't know what else.

I said I didn't approve of bull-fighting.

After that I couldn't think of anything else to contribute.

Which was quite unusual for me.

I had finished my gin and tonic and I felt hungry.

I needed some tea and toast.

Fast.

I sat in abject misery while they talked and talked.

Robert paid no further attention to me.

Perhaps he was fearful of betraying his affections in public.

Finally, Pol said it was time to go.

He came with us, somewhat to my surprise.

On the way to the bus-stop, we were startled to see a drunk veering towards us.

As he came nearer, he began to aim himself at Robert.

It was clear he intended to beat Robert up.

I was frozen with horror, as the drunk speeded up into a run.

Just before he reached Robert, however, he was intercepted by Pol.

She just stuck her arm out.

He ran straight into her arm and immediately collapsed.

She hadn't watched all those bull-fights for nothing. She did not hesitate.

Robert thanked Pol profusely for this service.

I thought it rather unladylike myself.

We decided to take a taxi at this point.

Robert said it would be easy for him to walk home from our place, and he wanted to see us safely home.

I found this somewhat awkward, as I am not used to having the object of my affection at such close quarters for so long, and I was developing the usual stomach ache.

In the end, he accompanied us straight into the flat.

And he did not leave that night.

As I went to sleep, I heard the customary clanking of the bed in Pol's room.

Clanks and moans.

Why does the reproductive act have to sound so tragic? I wondered.

I was feeling rather tragic myself.

How could Robert sink to Pol's level?

How could he settle for second-best?

And there was something else bothering me too.

Pol was supposed to be in love with ME.

I'd been trying to be kind to her on that account for the whole of the last month!

And now . . .

CLANKS AND MOANS.

My Hands on the Wall

I lay in bed.

Morose.

Clanking I could bear.

Moaning.

Laughing.

But I could not understand why he'd chosen Pol instead of me.

She was not perfectly beautiful.

Nor was I, of course.

I, with flakey skin on my heels and an old stain on my eye and knobbly knees and hardly any breasts to speak of and moles in places no polite person would mention, AND allergic to nuts.

I, who find it necessary to rearrange food in supermarkets if it's out of place.

I, who even rearrange matches inside their box so that they're all pointing in the same direction and more or less level.

But at least I was of a more normal size.

She was all flesh.

All wobbling flab.

And spirited bawdy talk.

She was just a Good Time Girl.

She was a lot of fun, yes, but how long can that sort of thing last?

I would have married him!

A virgin bride.

I would have had his babies.

I could envisage the scene.

Our children would have been beautiful, because we loved each other.

But my imaginings were interrupted by the sound of Pol moving about in the kitchen.

How disgusting, I thought.

She was always hungry after a night of love.

She was always having nights of love.

I don't know which disgusted me more.

Then I heard Robert yawn in the next room.

Just beyond the wall.

He was lying there.

Sleepy and stretching.

Robert, my love.

I knelt on my bed and outstretched my hands to him.

I put my hands on the wall in the place that I thought he might be, and left them there.

Feeling the wall in my hands.

Splutters to the Rescue

I was rather cold towards Robert at breakfast.

I was in no condition to be civil.

I was proud and aloof.

But I could not help noticing Robert's breakfast manner.

It was impeccable.

Somewhat less impeccable when Pol was sitting on his lap, however.

But that was understandable.

Given the size of her.

I finally admitted to myself that she was fat.

FAT, FAT, FAT.

And because she was on his lap, I had to reach for the marmalade myself at one point.

Luckily, my dressing-gown was done up tightly.

Even at times like these, I take care over such matters.

I have my pride.

Of course, I could not eat a thing.

But I made a brave show of preparing to eat.

I had in fact eaten very little in the last twenty-four hours.

At the Catafalque that morning, I nearly fainted.

I longed for eleven o'clock, when tea and toast could be obtained in the cafeteria, and the Splendid Young Man could be gazed at.

Although by now I was in love with Robert, primarily.

I liked Robert's stiffness at the breakfast table.

There was something manly about it.

His stiffness made him sit still a lot, looking meditative.

His unbendability made him spill his tea at times.

His elbows needed a lot of room, as they were incapable of adjusting to a tight spot.

It was charming.

His stiffness.

And now all was lost.

Pol recognized no seniority in my position, no prior claims.

She did not even know I HAD BEEN IN HIS STUDY.

She was probably in it now.

They were probably lying together among his books, in the very room where I had first met him.

Considering this possibility during Dr Splutters' Kant class, I burst into tears.

Though he was well-known for conveying the sentimental aspects of his subject, even Splutters did not believe I was crying over Kant.

After the class, Splutters insisted on taking me to a café and buying me a cream cake.

He was so kind, and so pathetic, as always, that I managed to give him a brief account of my troubles whilst eating the cream cake.

It did not take long, as I left out names and any reference to sex, and I was kept busy trying to eat the cream cake demurely.

When we walked back to the Catafalque, Splutters put a fatherly arm round my shoulders.

Although, never having had a father, I could only guess at what fatherliness involved.

Then he kissed me on the cheek.

This was too much.

My cheeks were sacred.

I was saving them for my husband.

I backed away.

He began to splutter on about how he'd long admired my eyes and my arms and what a joy it had been for him to have me in his classes these many months.

It was all very embarrassing and clearly no longer fatherly.

It only confirmed how strongly I felt for Robert.

I wasn't going to settle for second-best.

I ran towards the Catafalque.

Splutters ran after me, but to my relief he slowed his pace when he saw Sir Humphrey Basilisk coming out.

In Pol's Drawers

I soon became used to having Robert about the flat.

It was tantalizing.

For at any moment he might come to the conclusion that he and I were made for each other.

I often wondered if one day I might find him on MY bed, maddened by passion.

In fact, I checked the dark room for ghosts and for Robert every time I entered it.

I often thought Pol's men friends were using her.

They only wanted her for sex.

And as a companion to take to pubs and discos.

That was all they did together.

It seemed a pointless existence to me.

It was against my feminist principles.

It was against my feminine principles.

She was going to end up with some disease, despite the many varieties of condom she claimed to have in some drawer.

As well as in her handbag.

As if she might meet someone at any moment and need to go to bed with him there and then!

I didn't see any future in it for her.

Here she was, almost finished with her degree, and still no prospects of marriage on the horizon.

She was going about it the wrong way.

She was too easy.

She did not earn men's respect.

And she had so many men!

Why did she need mine?

This time it was the opposite problem: SHE was using HIM.

After a few weeks, she told me Robert was boring.

She wanted to get rid of him.

The next time he came round, I was supposed to tell him she was out.

The 33-year-old Woman's Selflessness

Robert came over quite early one morning, hoping to catch the worm.

I had always enjoyed his company at breakfast, so I invited him in.

Even when nervous, I can always produce some tea and toast.

Even in my dressing-gown.

We talked about Pol for some time.

When the question came up, I reported that she had stayed the night elsewhere.

And hinted that she must therefore be interested in someone else.

I felt it was best to warn him against wasting any more time on her.

He was simply being USED.

It was pure selflessness on my part.

I had no hopes left on my own account.

It was obvious enough that he did not love me.

I was just doing my job: Pol had told me to get rid of him.

He seemed somewhat crestfallen after this news.

So I made more tea and toast.

But now that he was no longer involved with Pol, I was feeling more jittery with him.

I started dropping things.

The toast, as if responding to my mood, popped high out of the toaster.

Suddenly I felt exhausted.

I was pooped.

It reminded me of my mother, slaving away to make a man happy.

I was relieved when he left.

Still Life with Cragshaw

The Splendid Young Man and his tennis court had galvanized the student body at the Catafalque Institute. Convinced of the merits of the scheme, they had decided to stage a pro-tennis court demo in the Gardens, and were already flattening the allocated spot with their posteriors.

Cragshaw, peeping from behind a blind, witnessed the gathering hordes. The prevailing winds were against him. He was outnumbered, outmanoeuvred – they were going to see him off the premises without a doubt. But they were going to have to kill him first. He could not bear being at home with his wife all day. Where would he sit? There was no room there for another slide. And somewhere in Cragshaw glimmered the knowledge, wise and irrefutable, that he himself was the only person in the world he didn't severely irritate.

No, it would not do. He would barricade himself in his quarters and see how they liked it. The newspapers would enjoy the scandal: 'Eminent Art Historian on Hunger Strike'. He could no longer concentrate on his work. After pinning a note to his door cancelling all classes for the day, he lay down in glum stupor under his table. There he noticed a small painting. He had no idea where it had come from but it looked rather like an early Chardin.

Our Heroine Makes Some Suppositions

I was hurrying towards Dr Cragshaw's rooms one day, in order to discuss borrowing some slides from him for my lecture in Lewes.

It was months away but I was already getting nervous about it.

And since my destiny was to love, but to love always tragically, I was determined to divert all my energy to my work.

I was about to knock on the door when I suddenly saw the two men in my life, Robert and Lionel, talking to each other beside a hedge.

I was extremely startled, and huddled against the wall until the two men in my life had wandered on.

I succumbed to day-dreams.

Supposing the Splendid Young Man/Robert was at the Catafalque late one night.

And I was too.

And we got locked in together!

Supposing I was completely at his (the Splendid Young Man's/Robert's) mercy.

Supposing he desired me fiercely, almost to the point of losing control of himself.

Supposing he took me in his arms, and then struggled to resist kissing me, but in the end could not help himself.

Supposing both Robert and Lionel Syms were at the Catafalque.

Supposing they BOTH wished to take me in their arms.

Supposing there was a fight.

I would weep and tell them to stop it.

Perhaps they would agree to share me.

. . . !

My thoughts on these and related matters were abruptly intruded upon when Robert popped his head round a bush and asked me to come to the pub with him that night.

Their First Date

I was dumbfounded.

I was thrilled.

I was amazed.

It was all so sudden.

He came to the flat at about seven and I was still washing up the supper things.

I said I would be ready to go as soon as I'd dried the dishes.

He said, 'Hey, Isabel, loosen up! We're only LIVING, you know. We don't have to take an exam at the end of it.'

'As far as we know,' was my rather witty reply.

So I washed and dried the dishes.

I do not trust the laws of physics to do a proper job.

I do not trust natural processes in general.

I do not like or trust these things.

Then something thrilling happened, something I had been waiting for all my life.

At a certain point in our walk towards the pub, Robert told me to take his arm.

'WHAT?' I gasped, unused to such requests.

'Take my arm,' he said again, quietly but insistently.

Manfully, if you must know.

So . . . I . . . did it.

Gently, ecstatically, but tremblingly and perhaps in

retrospect a little too tentatively but it is so difficult to gauge exactly what degree of feminine bashfulness is required at precise moments, I slipped my hand into the delicious and dangerous crook of Robert's elbow, and left it there.

Ecstasy.

The wonderful stiffness of his arm thrilled me, I knew not why.

We fitted together perfectly.

We were clearly made for each other.

Robert then explained that he had just spotted an ex-girlfriend across the street and wanted her to think he was involved with somebody.

It was so romantic.

I was very flattered that he might want to appear 'involved' with me.

I was completely overwhelmed.

It was perhaps the most romantic event of my life.

At the pub we had an argument.

I like a man I can argue with.

Robert said, 'There's a lot of history in big cities.'

I said, 'I don't like history. I don't like thinking about all those people who lived here before us. Except in historical novels.'

'All I said was, there's a lot of history in big cities,' said Robert rather grumpily.

Perhaps he was slightly offended that I never seemed to agree with him about anything.

But I felt that kept things exciting.

I went to get some more drinks, and was accosted by a man who asked me if I was Iris.

'What if I am?' I answered daringly.

That was how I was when I was with Robert.

He made me feel proud and defiant.

I was certainly much too proud to THROW myself at Robert, the way Pol had.

That seemed a meagre form of courtship to me.

I wanted Robert to have to use all his skill and cunning to win me.

And perhaps to take advantage of me one day when he happened to be overwhelmed with desire in an idyllic setting with the landscape unfolding beneath us.

I had always wanted a landscape to unfold beneath me.

I did not want to settle for second-best.

Unfortunately, Robert showed no signs of being overcome with passion.

After our date I felt very lonely.

I actually seemed to have been doing all the courtship by myself.

The tension before the date, the examination of every detail afterwards.

What he said, then what I said, then what he said.

This game is no fun unless two play.

Pregnant!

The Catafalque Institute, Purport Place, was in uproar.
Not only had Dr Cragshaw disappeared into his office,
permitting no one but his wife to bring him supplies. A new
and unexpected worry had arisen. One of the moral certainties of life at the Catafalque Institute, despite the uncertainty of everyone's morals, was the fact that the sole
member of the weaker sex to be allowed to teach there was
no longer of child-bearing age. Her much-envied absences
were tolerated with the strict understanding that they were
essential to her research and that, far from enjoying any
special privileges, she was actually paid less than anyone
else.

And now, without consulting anyone, without even
having the decency to reveal at her initial interview that
she was still fertile in body as well as in mind, Dr Lotus had
inexplicably become pregnant. At such a time, when the
Catafalque's funds were low and its standing in the academic world debatable, the esteemed scholars were faced
with the ghastly realization that Angelica Lotus would be
expecting maternity leave. The financial considerations
were in fact so pressing that it was a few more days before
anyone thought to enquire about Dr Lotus's marital status.
Unless she had been doing some research into this too, in
Vienna or elsewhere, it was doubtful whether the whole

matter could be kept from the press. All in all, the thing was not to be borne.

Splutters was given the task of hinting to Angelica Lotus that much as her colleagues acknowledged her intentions to be of the highest calibre, it was generally felt that she should investigate recent findings on the subject of severe abnormalities in the babies of middle-aged women. And that there were also known to be serious risks to the mother when giving birth so late in life.

This Splutters duly carried out, adding a touch of his own, to the effect that everyone had been much surprised by her sudden show of fecundity, as they had all assumed she'd given up the activity, not to say the hormones, required to produce such a state in herself, years ago. He politely offered his surprise that a woman should be having relations, particularly giving birth to any, so late in life.

'Is it so unseemly?' she asked, wearily. 'And if so, may I ask why you continue with YOUR varied sexual doings?'

'The general feeling, I'm afraid, is that it is all right for a man. It is natural for a man to remain active. As you know, WE can go on spreading our seed well into old age, touch wood.'

'You don't seem to be aware that middle-aged men are just as likely to produce damaged offspring as middle-aged women.'

'My dear woman, men do not usually indulge in the procreative act for the purposes of procreation! No, although I am often rather sorry to thwart the little devils. They surge so heroically towards their goal, the victor piercing his way into the egg in triumph . . . as it were. But one has responsibilities, doesn't one?'

'So I've noticed, Splutters,' replied Angelica darkly. 'By the way, this heroic victor of yours. Perhaps it's time someone straightened you out on the facts of life. The sperm is SELECTED by the egg. There is no race, no jousting competition. The egg decides which is the most genetically acceptable. YOU make it all sound like RAPE!'

At this point, Dr Lotus did something once again that was never done at the Catafalque (mainly because no one knew exactly how much shaking the building could take without crumbling to the ground). Though small, pregnant and usually quite kind, Dr Angelica Lotus slammed her door.

The Lotus Position

Angelica Lotus had been attracted in early adolescence, a formative age, to the opulent gold-mashed paintings of Gustav Klimt. The way a beautiful head would emerge from the gold for a kiss swept her off her feet. All her erotic urges focused themselves on Vienna from then on.

As a small child she had been an evacuee, thrown from a penny-pinching, formerly wealthy family (in which the main topic of conversation was the price of pork necks at Sainsbury's) into an even grimmer existence outside London. A bar of chocolate she'd received for the train journey was immediately taken away by the stern woman who was to look after her. 'Stole Angie's chocolate,' said the three-year-old to herself again and again until the fact became bearable. But other horrors followed. She was never given enough to eat, and was left outside every Saturday night while the woman went to the pictures. And this went on for years.

On her return home, it took three years for her to reach a normal size. By then she was fed up with mundane, rationed post-war Britain. She longed for forbidden fruit. She longed for the enemy. She finally went to Vienna to study Art History. There she met an ex-Nazi professor who taught her to enjoy being whipped. What could English Art Historians offer after that?

Vienna was a city built on artifice, male towers and

female domes topping the baroque *trompe-l'œil* churches. Every trick was played on the eye. Even the Danube had been swayed from its course, and its enigmatic waters were polluted. Angelica Lotus allowed herself only brief visits, for fear of breaking the city's fragile spell. She did not want to be left with a mess of meaningless Mozart records.

The Nazi had long since been supplanted by slightly more politically sound young men, undergraduates whom she hired to help her with her research. She liked men a little plump, so fed them up with chocolate cakes and creamy coffee until the effect on their bellies was evident. Then she seduced them with Klimt, tying them up in golden robes to the tune of Strauss waltzes, sung by the Vienna Boys Choir. Atmosphere was essential. Her sexual equipment was always left behind in her Vienna flat – she had no use for suspender belts and fetishistic leather gear during her London lethargies.

But now it was getting harder to pick up the students, and as she stiffened with age, she was tiring of ephemeral mystique and sins. She had decided on a child some time before managing to create one. But once she was determined, she found with ease an Adonis who was willing to be wined and dined and fattened up. He even turned out to possess a human cart, specially designed to be pulled by a woman (extra tackle to fit around breasts, etc.), and he knew how to use the whip.

During one of their outings through some remote woods, Angelica dared to look back at her master, sunning himself contentedly as the cart rolled him along. She was punished for this later. He fucked her lackadaisically, she came wildly and, to her menopausal body's eternal surprise, conceived.

The 33-year-old Woman's Unsuccessful Talk

I was sorry to hear that Dr Cragshaw had disappeared without trace.

I had hoped to borrow some of his slides for my lecture to the Workers' Educational Association in Lewes.

The Workers' Educational Association of Lewes turned out to consist of six people.

After my lecture which somehow lasted only ten minutes, I asked if they had any questions.

One person enquired if that had been only the first half of my talk.

Another asked why I hadn't brought any slides.

Then we adjourned to have some tea, which I was grateful for.

While I drank it, further complaints were expressed about my talk.

I had to admit I had read it rather fast.

I kept apologizing.

Meanwhile no one seemed the slightest bit interested in my thoughts on heterosexuality.

The Workers of Lewes are very demanding people.

Paris in the Spring: I

It was ecstatic.

It was heavenly.

It was all clearly leading up to something.

There had been many enjoyable, argumentative meetings.

Shy like teenagers, we had discussed our lonely lives.

He had told me of his career difficulties.

He had taken me to pubs.

He had introduced me to some of his friends.

He had made me take his arm once.

We had travelled in a taxi, just the two of us.

In the exquisite darkness of the taxi, we had scrupulously avoided touching each other.

A tantalizing occasion.

But I feared always that my dreams might be hopeless.

For instance, when he mentioned a pretty girl he had seen, or a beautiful one, I knew all was lost.

I couldn't compete on that level.

I did not want to hear about the beauties he had known in former days.

I, a 33-year-old virgin with increasingly dry skin on my knees and elbows.

I, a 33-year-old virgin addicted to rearranging the food on supermarket shelves.

I, with my limited command of philosophy.

I, ill-read, ill-made, prone to illness of all kinds.

And allergic to nuts.

I.

So I held back, however much I might have wished to catapult myself into Robert's arms.

Even the night he stayed and talked until three in the morning, I held back.

Well, I didn't want to lose my virginity at three in the morning!

That would certainly be settling for second-best, after so many years fraught with danger and heartache and similar decision-making.

Not that he made any attempt on my honour anyway.

He slept that night in Pol's bed.

Luckily, she wasn't in it.

It was May, and the dawn broke early.

I of course did not sleep a wink.

I hatched a plan instead.

The next day we were all setting off for Paris.

It was the annual Catafalque trip to see museums.

At breakfast I told Robert he should come along.

I said it would do him good.

I even admitted that it would not be fun without him.

I was that brazen about it.

I was feeling spirited and impulsive.

Reckless and obstinate.

But Robert did not do things on impulse.

He did not like sudden plans.

On impulse he had sold his entire collection of kitsch paraphernalia and come to England for a job that did not exist.

So I had to use all my feminine powers of persuasion.

It was pure selflessness on my part.

I could tell he needed a change of scene.

Paris in the spring.

So romantic.

The air alone would surely make him amorous.

I myself was quite amorous enough already.

Sleepless, almost speechless with it.

I was not, on the other hand, overly demonstrative.

I had heard somewhere that men feel easily overwhelmed by overly demonstrative women.

But even my undemonstrativeness had no effect.

He said no.

Paris in the Spring: II

Splutters had always enjoyed the annual expedition to Paris, where he could practise his French while making romantic headway with his students. There were long lunches together and evening strolls. It was a bonding experience, to show young women about a foreign city. Perhaps he would get a chance to be alone with Isabella at last – she had been neglecting him shamefully.

Splutters wasn't always chosen as one of the trip's supervisors, but this year he had insisted. Life at the Catafalque was becoming intensely uncomfortable for him. Not only was there no peace to be had in the Gardens, now that the tennis court was under construction, but Angelica Lotus was determined to antagonize him by pinning reports on the progress of her pregnancy on the Staff Room bulletin board. The latest had read simply, 'HEIGHT OF FUNDUS 12'.

Splutters was eager to start carousing, but after getting several of his most beguiling students sloshed on the ferry, he had unfortunately passed out himself, only regaining consciousness four hours later. His nausea turned out to be caused not by the boat but by the bus on to which he had been carried comatose and somewhat *déshabillé*. Mourning his lost opportunities, Splutters was the first to emerge later from his hotel room, ready for anything. The informality of the Paris trip excited him. The conjunction of his female students with the Eiffel Tower was almost too much to bear. In museums, he would gently encircle a student with his arm, his sleeves jauntily rolled up, and lead her towards a secluded painting. If a slight thrill, whether of aesthetic or sexual pleasure, seemed to have been evoked thus, he was liable to follow her around for the rest of the morning in the hopes of securing a seat beside her at lunch. Students had an unlikeable tendency to form a giggly gang. It was therefore essential to isolate one's prey.

Paris in the Spring: III

It was ecstatic.

I was ecstatic.

I had given up all hope.

And then he came!

Robert turned up at Victoria Coach Station at the last minute to join the Catafalque Paris expedition.

He sat next to me on the bus.

Well actually, he sat next to the Splendid Young Man, but they were just across the aisle from Pol and me.

Of course no other man could ever seem attractive to me, now that Robert's face was engraved on my memory.

But it was wonderful to have the two men in my life sitting so close.

Robert, Pol, Lionel and I had beefburgers together on the ferry.

As you can imagine, I was overwhelmed.

It was so romantic, and we hadn't even reached Paris yet!

I was bewilderingly happy.

Perhaps Robert was bewildered too.

I thought at one point that he might be about to kiss me.

We were standing by a porthole, and he leaned forward as if he was trying to look out, but the glass was too smudgy.

It was a remarkable moment.

At the hotel, he and Lionel shared a room.

I shared with Pol.

We went round with the whole Catafalque crowd all day.

It was heavenly.

Although such togetherness made it rather hard to get a cup of coffee.

Splutters often seemed to be following me about, but after we'd seen the Pompidou, Robert and I went off on our own for a walk.

We had hardly gone further than a few streets away when someone grabbed me by the neck and pulled me into a dark, narrow alleyway.

At first I hoped it might be Robert, suddenly overcome with desire.

But then I saw that he too was being dragged along by two men wearing berets.

There were three of them altogether, and they all wore berets.

They tied us up, back to back.

It was rather romantic.

They went through our pockets and took all our money.

And then they ran off.

Of course I was crying.

But I soon stopped.

I realized that if I went on I would need to blow my nose and that would be difficult with my hands tied behind my back.

And it was a joy, after all, to be in such miraculous proximity to my love, even though he was wiggling about rather irritatingly.

I felt him warm against me.

If only I could turn my head enough, perhaps he would kiss me.

All of a sudden he jumped up, and turned to release me from my bonds.

He said he had studied Houdini's methods.

He was able to escape from almost any knot.

I looked at him with wonder and admiration.

My saviour.

Who beneath his stiff bearing had been studying Houdini all along.

Whose stiffness, I had always hoped, might some day soften into tenderness.

Paris in the Spring: IV

Pol wasn't sure why, but she found she fancied Splutters in Paris. His predatory air turned her on in the new surroundings. Instead of looking at paintings, she watched his progress with women. At supper that night she sat by him. She needed something to entertain her. She was tired of Syms's arrogance. She was tired of watching Isabel and Robert making eyes at each other. She put a hand between Splutters' thighs and whispered in his rather hirsute ear, 'Don't you know I bloody fancy you? What the fuck are you going to do about it?'

Splutters choked and was led away somewhere by one of the waiters. Pol proceeded to eat his *rognons*, which he had ordered by accident, having tried to say *oignons*. His accent was not what it had been.

Paris in the Spring: V

That evening, we all had supper together at a large restaurant.

I was sitting across from Lionel and Robert.

It was heavenly.

Until Pol turned up and sat down between them.

She put her fat arms around both the men in my life, and began to pick at their suppers.

Then she said, 'Ugh! this mussel's off.'

Robert and I had both ordered mussels because we thought it was the thing to do in Paris.

I didn't think they were that bad.

What troubled me much more than the mussels was the depressing amount of fondness for Pol which I detected in both Lionel's and Robert's eyes.

When she went to the loo, they watched her until she was out of the room.

Could it be that Robert still pined for her?

The thought was horrifying.

And was it possible that the Splendid Young Man, firm in mind and body, the idol of everyone at the Catafalque and beyond, in fact the Platonic ideal, could wish to sully his soul and other more material aspects of his persona, with the likes of Pol?

My feeling was that he could have done better.

Much better.

This was pure selflessness on my part.

I no longer had any intention of troubling him with my attentions.

Robert was the man for me.

We had been through a bonding experience together, Robert and I, when we were tied up by those thieves.

Ever since, I had been wondering whether he might have kissed me if we had been tied up for a little longer.

And besides that, I still had the delicious and tantalizing memory of his tentative movement towards me when we were by the porthole.

Pol returned and we all left for an evening promenade by the Seine.

The lights of Paris at night were truly twinkling.

The only problem was that almost as soon as we reached the river, I fainted.

It was very romantic.

I think Robert was one of the ones who caught me.

I had just said to Pol, 'I don't feel very well.'

And then I fainted.

When I awoke, I was sitting on the pavement, with Pol, Lionel and Robert circled around me.

I immediately wondered if it had been a dainty fall.

Robert, gratifyingly, seemed particularly flustered by the event.

In fact, as soon as I was on my feet again, he began to hyperventilate himself.

He said he thought he was having some kind of heart attack.

(All because of me!)

Pol was very worried about him.

Although she no longer cared for him personally, she considered him a great Art Historian.

She made me run and get a taxi.

I told the driver to take us to the hospital, in my faltering French, whilst pointing at my chest.

'*Le coeur?*' he asked.

I didn't know what he was talking about so Pol handled the rest, plonking herself down in the front seat.

Robert sat between me and Lionel in the back.

I patted Robert's hand.

I tried hard to empathize with his suffering.

I did not want to live if he died.

And soon I was gasping for breath myself.

My heart seemed to be exploding.

My hand, which had been patting his, went limp.

I felt him clasp it, but I was far, far away.

My soul seemed to want to drift out of the window.

I had to keep reminding myself to live.

Robert pressed my hand and said something encouraging, but I knew we were dying.

I did not want to die without telling him I loved him.

But I was incapable of speech.

I turned to him.

He looked down at me.

His face was near.

So . . . I . . . kissed him.

He seemed to kiss me back.

At last we understood each other.

Now, when it was almost too late.

I surrendered myself utterly to the magic and enchantment of his lips.

Though not for long, as we were both out of breath and apparently having heart attacks.

After our kiss, I lay my head on his shoulder.

At last.

It had been said.

We loved each other.

There was nothing more I needed to do in life.

I could have died happy.
I would have died very happy.
But we survived.

'Foetal Heart Heard'

It seems that it was the mussels.

After a few hours at the hospital, we were sent back to our hotel.

The future seemed certain and bright.

But we were very tired.

I was pooped.

I was worried about my hair.

And I needed to get to a loo quickly.

We parted listlessly in the corridor.

And met again the next morning, at breakfast.

Pol immediately reported to Robert that I had spent most of the night on the loo.

He admitted he had too.

Pol said, 'Well, I've heard of togetherness, but this is ridiculous. First you were mugged, now you've both got diarrhoea!'

She cackled for some time.

It was a relief when she left the table.

I was not feeling totally comfortable.

For once in my life, I had not had the strength to rinse out my Janet Reger knickers the night before.

I had had to borrow some of Pol's.

They were not Janet Reger.

Janet Reger does not make knickers that big.

127

They were by Marks & Sparks and I had to do them up with a safety-pin.

So I was suffering from various indignities as I contemplated my love across the table.

I felt sorry for Pol in a way.

She would probably never know what it is like to meet the man you are to marry, in a Parisian café, the morning after a near-death experience.

We were a little shy together at first, laughing sheepishly about our adventures.

Then we made small talk about Paris.

Alone at last.

Feeling fragile.

Pooped.

And very much in love.

There was a pregnant pause.

Then Robert spoke.

'Well,' he said, 'that's the last time I eat mussels.'

That broke the ice a bit, but I could not help wondering who would be the first to admit that bad mussels had not been the only cause of our irregular heart-beats.

That love had played its part.

That we had nearly died of love, in fact.

As Robert went on to speak of his health purely in technical terms, I saw that it would have to be me that brought up the true significance of the event.

It was a little while before I could think of a delicate way of putting it.

Finally, I said, bashfully, 'Robert, I hope you didn't think I was sexually molesting you in the taxi.'

That was bound to provoke a firm denial and an even firmer declaration.

Or so I thought.

But he merely said, 'Oh, that was just like two people clinging in the snow.'

Well, I have my pride.

I excused myself and went to the loo.

It was a porcelain hole in the ground, and I vomited into it.

Two people huddling together in the snow as they die.

A relationship based on happenstance and necessity.

Our moment of greatest understanding was to him just the result of a medical emergency.

He had filed the incident under 'Kisses Received When Unable to Refuse'.

He had denied our love.

I looked at my worn-out face in the mirror.

The stain on my left eye.

The hair that fails to come to life in the sun.

I cupped my breasts in my hands, as heroines are supposed to do when in front of mirrors.

It was hopeless.

Paris in the Spring: VI

The Splendid Young Man took Pol to Fontainebleau one evening. He was determined to rekindle their affair. It was the only reason he'd come on this silly Paris trip. They sat in an outdoor café and drank red wine. He talked to her of many things. Despite his obvious defects, she had to admit that this was better than her recent attempt to discuss Kant with Splutters.

They walked among the trees until dusk.

Then he pushed his tongue into her mouth.

He took her saggy-baggy breasts in his hands.

He licked her purple cunt until she opened for him.

They fucked until they both saw stars.

This indicated that it was night-time.

They sensibly proceeded back to the train station.

Exit Robert, Pursued by a Bear

While Isabel longed to tell Robert she loved him before she died, Robert had been worrying rather more about the after-life than whether or not he was loved in this one. He was not concerned at that moment about his place in her heart. He was afraid of losing his place in the whole scheme of things. Her kiss had astounded and frightened him. All in all, she seemed a rather dangerous woman. The first time he'd met her he thought she was a burglar. The next time, a drunk had tried to beat him up. Now he had been assaulted, tied up and robbed, and later involved in a near-death experience after following Isabel's advice on what to order at a restaurant.

All in all, it was not the worst of times to be offered a lucrative job back home. When he got back to London, under the usual letter from his mother detailing her health problems was an official envelope from the large and famous university based in his home town. Robert wasn't certain he wanted to return to his old home town – he'd gone to some trouble to escape it fifteen years before. But he'd been in London for some time without being offered any steady form of employment. The American in him felt a failure on this account.

And he'd recently had that fright. He felt like seeing his mother. He thought he should give the lucrative job a whirl for a trial period. He was sure that he wouldn't last long in America, though. He would miss his London life, his flat, his friends. Yes, and he would miss Isabel. Elusive though she was, he had grown attached to Isabel. Eating toast and drinking tea with her had for some time been the high point in his life.

But he wasn't prepared for all that blue sky. With jet lag he woke up at five or six in the morning and went outside to find a sky that was unreservedly, undeservedly blue. It was not an economical, stingy pastel-shaded sky. It reminded him of the translucence of Isabel's eyes. He revelled in it. He walked. He found he even liked the street names, the plain and simple ones like Central Street that hid nothing, and the more eccentric like Henry B. Goodrich III Avenue, which must have once meant something, to a limited number of people. It was all so familiar, it touched an ancient soft spot in his soul. He even liked the way the trash looked lying on the grass. The type of trash.

He realized suddenly that it was American women he was destined to love. They looked real to him. They were the women he'd seen as a boy and assumed he would one day marry. They were what women should be. Their voices sprang at him in crowds, their tans and the straight hair that fell like Niagara down their backs. And their lack of reserve, which softened his.

And his mother, who had always been ill, been ill and needed him and not needed him, was ill now and needed him. She was so glad he'd come home – she assumed, for good. Her love was different from the love of a holiday mother who knows your departure is imminent. He needed her like this. He needed it all. Why had he done without it for so long, punished and deprived himself? He'd been continually half-starved of love by the British, who can live on small quantities of the stuff. He even enjoyed the gift-bearing neighbours, who came over with Welcome Home coffee cakes. He suddenly wanted to be succoured and enveloped by love.

The terrible truth that he hadn't dared admit to himself since the Vietnam war was that he was proud of his country, and of California in particular. As a child, a miserable child, he had known that California was the centre of the world. Lassie lived in California. Mr Ed probably lived in California. California had it all. Snow-capped mountains and glacial lakes. Waterfalls, earthquakes, the Pacific. It had a Spanish Colonial past, and native Indians. Mountain goats, red squirrels, white-tailed and black-tailed deer, elk and antelope, grizzly, brown and cinnamon bears, gophers and woodpeckers and roadrunners, mocking-birds, vultures, eagles, sea-turtles and whales. It had oranges, grapes, peaches, plums, prunes, cherries, pomegranates, avocados, olives, almonds and walnuts. Sequoias and cacti. Oil, copper, gold, diamonds, topazes as blue as Isabel's eyes, quartz, coal, mercury, Borax and nitrate of soda. What else could he require?

Moreover, his mother was ill, old and frail. He had never seen her like this. And what had he to return to in London? A mess of dead-end feelings for Pol. His many attempts, failed and various, at love. And Isabel, who sometimes shuddered, sometimes stuttered, but never never revealed herself to him. Was he expected to go to England on the off-chance that a few of her tenderer tremors were on his behalf? And he was still smarting over her avoidance of him in Paris after that terrible night. All along, she had given him the sort of On-Off treatment scientists use to drive rats insane. In humans, this merely leads to a state of high anxiety. She was a mystery to him. A mystery banana.

California, and his place in it, seemed straightforward. And it just happened to be beautiful. And his mother just happened to live there. And it just happened to have on Special Offer today, a lucrative academic job.

How many innocent lives have been sacrificed for less?

Shit!

Down, down in the bowels, down in the basement of the Catafalque sit the dregs of society who consider themselves the crème. They coagulate in the cafeteria, they know not why. Everyone was treating each other with little care, and being treated with little care. Ours is not a romantic world.

Down, down in the basement of the Catafalque Institute sat Isabel, reading a letter from Robert. But it wasn't exactly a letter. It was a change of address card.

Our Hero Regresses

It was by chance he met his first love in the local super-market. His mother had sent him to get a few things they could just heat up. She (and he) loved things that could just be heated up. And there was Gail, her delicate hand, still delicate though bigger, fingering a box of cookies. Causing Robert to reflect that in all the days of their romance twenty years before, they had never made love. This seemed a bit of an omission. He pushed his trolley towards her.

Perhaps she's the One, the only one for me.

My one and only.

He introduced himself near the beans. Barbecue Beans, Boston Beans, Franks 'n' Beans. He dimly observed that the beans were in alphabetical order before she noticed, recognized and kissed him.

She let his agedness pass without comment, as he did hers. They had both become more substantial figures since they'd last met. Their bones had grown.

He was undone.

Ann Donne.

John Donne.

Undone.

Everything in California seemed sensual to him.

Even Gail, against a row of beans.

He liked the smell of her.

He liked the weekend smell of her later as he loosened the sheets of her bed.

Gail received him nimbly, deftly, as a California woman should.

Her vagina was tight as an acrobat's, her breasts were firm rounded pyramids, as they should be.

She was tanned all over, except where she shouldn't be.

The past could be recovered this easily.

To open an old trunk and find everything improved, more useful than before.

Now, that's an achievement.

Our Hero Feels Inspired

Sensual Gail and California.

Robert felt inspired.

Gail would be his muse.

He took the idea of her love out on walks and thought up topics for his lectures.

He noticed trees.

They seemed to be in agony.

Their branches begged for help, as tormented roots ground their way through rocky soil.

It was agony made beautiful.

Like Gail when she came, loud like a California girl should.

Why did humans build angular shapes to live in, plonking squares and rectangles down on the ground everywhere they went?

He wanted to write a new treatise on beauty, a new Serpentine Line.

Nothing approaches the grace of a tree clinging to a cliff, unseen for a thousand years.

And Gail.

Gail was clean and beautiful and familiar, like an old wooden bench beaten soft and warm by time.

Gail was also into computers.

She also had long blond hair that came to life in the sun.

He loved that hair.

He had always hoped, without thinking about it, that he would one day have and hold a woman with such hair.

All of which got a little less alluring as the months wore on and the complexities of computing were thoroughly explained to him.

But he liked Gail.

He was fond of Gail.

In fact, though they had less and less to say to each other, it never occurred to either of them that they were not in love.

Gail's Mother

The author feels no interest in Gail or her mother at the
present time.

6,000-mile Abyss

Robert had hesitated before telling Isabel about Gail. It was a serious step to take, perhaps a final step. But since he was fucking Gail every weekend, he wasn't sure he should be hesitant. He broke the news in a letter accompanying the manuscript of his lecture on the relation of architecture to botanical structures, which he thought she might find interesting. He was quite proud of it.

A terrible silence ensued. Not a molecule of their writing paper fell on the lonely Atlantic for months. She didn't write, for fear of exposing her pain; he, to avoid her anger. He knew by her silence that she was angry. He had never known Isabel either silent or angry before. He had told her too much, lost her for ever, he thought one night sitting up late in his mother's house, and it chilled him.

How tenderly she handled his manuscript. Isabel, who had hidden her feelings for fear that they would overwhelm him, was not to know how much the poor fellow had wanted to be enveloped by love, how he had in fact travelled to the other side of the earth in the vague hope of being thus enveloped. Had taken himself home to beautiful Californian women, to his maniacally ill but still extant mother who in prehistory had so well regulated his body clock that in adulthood he always felt sleepy at three in the afternoon without knowing why.

Bananas

They had become exceedingly close.

She was no doubt exceedingly beautiful.

HE, who was too stiff to get close to anyone!

He, whose stiffness I had hoped to mould to fit my own.

His stiffness.

They say you should tell a man you love him if you do.

But I thought he knew.

Everything had seemed so certain, after all of our bonding experiences.

It was inevitable that we would eventually come together.

And now it was too late to do anything.

Who was I to alienate a man's affections from another woman?

I was nothing if not noble.

Selfless.

And resigned.

I had all the British virtues.

I was in love with my own pathos.

I was in despair.

I was fainting, freezing, dying from lack of love.

Even the 391 novels of Babs Cartwheel could not sustain me.

I was carrying home some bananas when it finally

occurred to me that Robert must be sleeping with this girl.

The bananas fell to the ground.

I stepped on them by accident, and started to cry.

I, Isabel, blubbered over bananas.

A few women stopped and offered to help me.

I shooed them away.

I stood against a wall, my feet in banana, and blubbered.

Having a horror of contact with the dead, with childbirth, with menstruous women, with murder whether wilful or involuntary, with almost any form of bloodshed, with persons or animals of inferior caste, with dead animal refuse, e.g. leather or excrement, with leprosy, madness and any form of disease, I performed my abultions with care.

My hands against the wall.

Playboy of the Western World

His home town was tumultuously dull for Robert, who had a horror of dullness. But it was a dullness he knew so well that it was part of him. Gail too was proving a bore. She was a product, a consumer product, of her times. She went shopping. What could be the purpose of this constant shopping, he wondered. The clothes certainly weren't bought for his delectation. They were something to do with her social set, her vast network of friends which spoke so glaringly of the years he'd been away: he hardly knew any of them. And he hardly wanted to.

Gail wasn't so sure she wanted him to either. She reserved some of the male friends for herself alone. After the first glow of reunion had worn off, she began to notice how un-Californian Robert was, and this seemed to her a fault. He was weak, lethargic and prone to colds despite the sunny clime. He seemed to believe he was mortally ill or something. Gail was not used to such symptoms in a man. The only real point of common ground seemed to be that she fitted his notion of ideal womanhood. But was he her ideal man?

So, here he was in the bosom or perhaps the hunky right thigh of America, surrounded by his mother and his first love, soon to begin a job he was eminently suited for, and Robert was not happy. He felt ill. He lounged about indoors, hiding from the ridiculous heat behind the protection of air conditioners. Lying in darkened rooms, roused by TV, he realized he was becoming his mother. He ate mid-morning a meal that sufficed for breakfast and lunch. And he tried to write his book on Giotto. People said this part of California was very like Tuscany, but he didn't believe it. He felt very far away from Europe. He remembered a card trick that had gone particularly badly, cards tumbling all over his family. His whole life was like that card trick, he thought, as he shuffled through the house. 'The Boomerang Card'.

He met a few old friends from high school for a beer and tried to talk to them about something of mutual interest. But he knew nothing of baseball. He was beginning to feel appalled by the tastelessness, confusion and endless foreignness of his native land. Others have gone back, he knew, gone back to their old home towns and settled right back in. But within months of leaving the dishevelled streets of London, the disabling weather, the useless bathroom showers, the snobbery, the yobbos, he missed them. He was too old to adjust to the different sort of seediness of a culture he half-remembered having yearned to escape from years ago.

He despaired of himself. He'd given up a healthy amount of struggle and despair in London for this weak and shameful retreat from the world. He did not even have his own place to live. He missed his flat, in which he had finally got everything the way he wanted it. He had taken pride in that. And now look at him. Home to Mommy. He'd forged his way into a new country and now voluntarily given it all up. Given up that dream for this dream. Given up a new dream for his oldest dream. And the point of the exercise? There were no arms after all eager enough to enclose him here. He'd taken on Gail to appease a need for warmth instilled in him by Isabel.

He kept getting colds. His shoulders ached. He could not relax. He needed a massage. Gail stretched him out with professional skill, doused him with perfumed oils warmed in her palm, and rubbed him down. This excited her but not him. It made him feel warm and loved. He did not dare ask for it again. Gail didn't like him sleepy and impotent, and she was fierce when roused.

All hope rested on his job. There he would make friends with people who were more on his wavelength. There he would feel part of the academic world. There he would be able to focus again on the things that mattered to him, instead of this nonsense of returning to the past, this ridiculous revisiting of childhood minus the hamsters and train sets. The plaid pyjamas.

What he needed was a new toy, an adult toy to fill the void. A car, obviously. His own car would make him feel less directionless. He went to a second-hand car dealer that a friend of Gail's had recommended. A vast car lot, with thousands of cars! He had never seen anything like it. He was definitely in a foreign country. And what he wanted was something small. No, maybe something fifties-ish, huge and phallic. But that was nostalgia again, which he had vowed to do without. He was trying to get a handle on the NOW. He did not need that old a car.

He looked at the Toyotas and Hondas, nice little cars. He knew something about cars, although he'd never considered getting one when he lived in London. This thought entailed a pang of regret. He couldn't help thinking that where he really wanted to be at that moment was not in the middle of a thousand Californian cars, but on a tube train going round and round on the Circle Line as he'd done when he first arrived in London and couldn't figure out where to get off. A dark, dank, dirty old tube train full of sullen sour English people avoiding eye contact, studying each other's footwear and vaguely envious of each other's newspaper.

He stood with hundreds of dollars in his pocket and a longing in his heart to buy a car, and couldn't. It was hopeless. Gail would yell at him for his incompetence but in the end she would come up with somebody's brother's car which would no doubt be a nice old car and a lot cheaper. He had wanted to go off and buy his own car in his own way in his own time. But the Gail way would probably be better.

Americans tend to see Europe in three weeks. It's a small place to them. People were always asking Robert how many countries he'd covered there. And every time he mentioned Paris, he was forced to think of his pathetic, aborted play for Isabel. He wondered if her virginity had yet succumbed to some other guy's onslaught. But then he reminded himself that Isabel talked non-stop and stuttered over the names of philosophers. He reminded himself that she had no breasts to speak of. He tried to forget her dazzling blue eyes, which she would have kept permanently shut had she known how beautiful they were. She was so obsessively PRIM.

So he languished, he faltered, he longed. And he rebuked himself daily for it.

Longing for a Man

I, Isabel, was having trouble getting to the Catafalque.

I, Isabel, was having trouble getting out of bed.

Occasionally, I drank gin and tonics until I could not even find my bed.

My grief lacked charm of any kind.

I quite liked writing to Robert from my position of powerlessness.

I wrote semi-mournful letters and got stiff replies.

I had always liked his stiffness.

He made me feel so feminine and vulnerable.

Especially now that he had abandoned me.

The thing about longing for a man.

Any man.

The longer you long for a specific one, the more unrequited you begin to feel about the whole lot of them.

An impassable barrier arises between you and them, which you cross by means of day-dreams.

Diverse visions of male splendidness beset me in my torpor.

Men in still shots.

Posed and handsome.

Snapshots of men.

Details of men.

Single brushstrokes of men.

I, Isbabel, no longer knew what I required of a man.
They had all become equally promising.
The Splendid Young Man's neck.
Robert laughing.
Splutters, naked, pouncing on me.
They will ALL do in the end.

Romp in a Hotel

He held my hand.

He wore a troubled expression.

Sometimes his mouth quivered as if he might burst into tears.

'Finish it,' I said.

I was determined to end our affair before it had begun.

'I don't do this sort of thing,' I murmured, without conviction.

Holding my hand in a hotel, Splutters spoke of his past.

His melancholy past.

His nanny, who had left him to become a games mistress.

His difficult, unfortunate, regrettable misalliance with The Wrong Woman, to whom he was still married.

It was too funny.

I erupted in helpless merriment.

In the room he'd booked he gently tried to undo my dress with the one little button at the neck.

And failed.

Then he tugged at it.

He chased me round the bed.

It was like a scene from some Swedish film about doctors and nurses.

Saucy Sisters, Vaccinating Vixens, Heart-Throb Hospital.

He was unwilling to forgo the pleasure of removing my green dress with the single button at the neck.

When I pulled away from him, he lunged across the bed to catch the hem of my dress and pull me to him.

He was very strong.

There was a definite possibility of being ravished quite soon by the wrong man.

It was shameful to tease Splutters.

It was not that I fancied him.

I did not love or respect Splutters, either as a tutor or as a man.

I did not even much like him.

I didn't care for the construction of his flaccid lips.

And every time he turned away from me, his back view looked like a girl's.

None the less, I enjoyed consorting with him.

I liked pretending that I was in his power.

As in all those Sheik books.

I had to admit that I, Isabel, suffer from Rape Fantasies.

These did not fit in too well with my feminist principles.

Which tended to merge with my prudish principles.

I was somewhat confused.

I was shocked by my own indecorous behaviour.

I managed to get out of the room, my dress and honour still intact.

This had in fact proved reassuringly easy.

Splutters' Nanny

Although his close encounters with Isabel demoralized and debilitated him, Splutters was ready for any amount of unconsummated arousal if only to be allowed to touch the object of his desire. He was used to rebuttal, anyway, and thrived on it. He had long known himself to be repulsive to the opposite sex, and he approached women with an open mind. From an early age, sexual excitement had been a one-sided affair.

Whatever the weather, his nanny had always insisted on bringing the umbrella when they went out walking. There was a good reason for this. She made him hold up the umbrella to hide her when she needed to pee. His only hope on their endless walks together was that she would need to use the umbrella in this way. He could hear the pissing sound as she crouched on the ground. The sight of an umbrella had remained a powerful stimulus for him ever since.

His nanny was heedless of the turmoil into which her micturation threw the young Splutters. His curiosity, obvious enough, had seemed to her merely innocent curiosity. As a result of which, he also found female displays of ignorance intensely exciting, which is why he had become a professor of Art History. Isabel, with her titters and her consternation, produced in him a perpetual state of priapic discombobulation. They both found each other's hotel room manner strangely satisfying. But they had even more in common than that. Little did they know that it was actually Splutters' nanny who had caused Isabel's ping-pong accident, resulting in the stain on her left eye. The nanny, now a games mistress and increasingly severe, had yelled at Isabel for being too slow, and Isabel, attempting to move too fast for her own good, fell and nicked her eye on the edge of the ping-pong table.

A Decline in Relations

Within months of Robert's return, his mother was in the hospital. She had inexplicable pains which the doctors, as ever, were determined to investigate. Until your heart finally stops beating, they talk as if a cure could be achieved.

Robert tactlessly brought grapes, forgetting that she was on liquids only, with a glucose drip in her arm. He did not want to get too involved in all this. It was an aspect of the past he hadn't wanted to revisit. Even at his most nostalgic, he wanted no part of hospitals.

He comforted himself with Gail. They heated things up together in the evenings. Gail didn't prod or pry. She didn't want to know. They didn't talk about his mother. Gail was the antidote to all that, something totally separate.

When his mother got out of the hospital, she was too weak to walk from the car to the house. He wondered if he was too weak to carry her. But he did. He carried her upstairs to her bedroom and helped her into her nightgown. He could be kind now. She feared he would quail at the sight of her poor old mutilated body. But Robert had always known that the mother he hugged needily was rotten with decay. A body as familiar as his own. He loved her still. He was gentle with her nakedness and made her comfortable in bed.

But her weakness went on and on. 'Illnesses are sent to try us,' she murmured absently. And it was true, he thought. His love, his patience, his moral health were all on trial. She began to smell and wouldn't let him wash her. He did not tell her she smelled, but the smell made him despair. It made him lose faith in himself. The miserable smell of her neglected flesh repulsed him. It was the smell of helplessness, the smell of cancer, the smell of these worries. It made him resent having to help her. With more than his usual stiffness he would put her slippers on her limp feet, walk her over to the commode, lift the nightgown and lower her down. Afterwards he would have to empty the pail. He ground his teeth in exasperation with it all.

It was his duty not to let her see his disgust and despair. But he could not do this if he had to smell that smell every day. He hired nurses. He had an excuse – his job. His mother didn't like the nurses. She did not believe that there was anything about her body any more that warranted their thoroughness.

She got sicker and sicker, and there was no time to recover from one sign of deterioration before there was another to grasp. It was all part of a pattern, the pattern of annihilation. And the smell was the smell of death. Contrary to public belief, the pallor and the stink of death actually precede it. They come in waves, in glimpses, in overpowering stenches, long before.

Our Hero's Job

He tried to carry on with his work. But he felt paralysed by indifference. Art meant nothing, nothing at all. He did not know what he was talking about, and wondered if he ever had. It was quite a predicament: at last he gets a job but has no will to teach. Whether or not paint had ever been spread across a single white surface touched no chord in him. It merely peeved him that people wasted his energy on such matters.

He could handle the disgruntlement of his students, who would no doubt malign him irreverently in the university magazine. But his competitive colleagues, having heard that Robert's mother was dying, were on the look-out for every omission, error or misdemeanour. Professional headway could be made by discrediting Robert for cancelling classes or not getting in on time.

He admired the doctors for their comparative dedication. They try to keep you entertained, do a test here, a test there. They yanked his mother on to stretchers, poked her with needles and tubes (forks and knives, for all he knew), investigated her with all manner of rays. He watched them show gentleness, until he wept, to a woman who had become for him a barely recognizable rag-bag of ailments. They did not give up on her, he was grateful for that. The hospital doors were opened wide for her. She was wheeled around like a grand piano, this rag-bag who could still sometimes hold his hand fondly (though the tired and the dying care about no one).

Contrary to Public Belief

Contrary to public belief, the world is not beautiful, lit by its ceiling light. Its design is flawed. Every living thing creates more mess than it picks up. We're transforming stations: we consume things that originally looked and smelled fairly good, and turn them into shit. This is our contribution to the universe.

We sleep a third of our lives away, and fuck if we're lucky about 5,000 times. Every day the whole show starts rolling again, all totally without significance. There can be no true tragedy or true joy in a world that is so repetitive. We try to fill these credibility gaps with painting, bits of ordered chaos; and music, noises hung on a line to dry. And love.

Robert was thinking about the relative importance of art and life when he was tapped on the arm by the Librarian, a stranger with an alliterative name. To be taken by the arm in a public place by a stranger with an alliterative name as if she wants to introduce you to someone, she gently takes you through the throng and out into a narrow, blankly lit hallway without shadows where there is no room, NO ROOM to writhe or explode or dissolve into grey sludge on the floor. There, her hand on his shoulder, she told Robert his mother had died.

She gave him a brandy. She told him of the end of the world and offered a drink as consolation.

The Librarian avoided him afterwards. She felt hideously bonded to him by his wails, and kept away.

Hot Potatoes

Amazing how you fill your pockets with hope on a cold day. How, when his life collapsed, Robert thought of Isabel. As he rushed to the hospital to search his mother's body for signs of life the doctors might have missed. As he held back from it in the end, his cold, motionless mother with a smear of food on her cheek. As he stood there surveying the little person he had tried to hold above water for so long, so vulnerable and now lost for ever because he had somehow tired of the task. And though the world caved in on Robert in his sad and silent fury. And though it offered no chance of atonement. Though he sought to concentrate fully for once on the moment at hand, the horror and the pain of it and his own uselessness. Though he even tried to busy himself with forms and arrangements and what little he knew of bereavement etiquette. Though the nurses offered sympathy and the doctors explanations, all of which he mutely accepted. Though he was finally drowning and content to drown in the whiteness of hospitals and their tasteless bustle. Though all this effort was required just to face the first few moments of knowing that the most important person was dead, yet, all this time his mind was full of Isabel. Six foot deep in the grey sludge of death, he clung to the raft that was Isabel.

He thought suddenly that he wanted to marry Isabel,

and this simple phrase kept going through his head. The timing of the sentiment appalled him. Its inappropriateness was almost amusing: 'Uh, hi, Isabel. My mother just died. Wanna get married?' It all seemed a touch callous, a tad mad.

But that's how you fill your pockets with hot potatoes on a cold day.

Important Advice

Gail insisted on coming over to clean up the house on the morning of the funeral. He watched her put the dirty dishes in the dishwasher and switch the thing on. She said it would be worse for him to return to a load of dirty dishes.

But Gail was wrong. Clean dishes are out of place in a world that is a shambles, a disgrace. People take your tragedies and try to make a nonsense of them with domestic detail.

At the reception, a friend told Robert he ought to laugh at himself more. You'd think burying your mother would be excuse enough to stop laughing for a while. But apparently this skill has to be kept in good working order at all times.

The smug self-containment of friends when you need them. Their incessant hold on reason, when life is behaving unreasonably. When you feel like a caged animal left to claw itself, pulling tufts of fur out and chewing its own tail and toes off in rage, disgust, despair, they tell you to laugh at yourself more.

Our Hero's Sister Sandy

Sandy attended the funeral but not the dying business. She had drunk Coke in the wilderness of Wyoming awaiting that death. She didn't go to watch her mother's decline, to hold her hand, to have her heart-strings pulled by that woman at the last. But she came to the funeral. She had a few things to pick up.

Sofas

Robert sat on sofas. He sat on sofas and tried to see what it feels like for your life to be over. He sat on sofas in a room and felt alone and dead. Utter stillness in the room. No one knowing he's sitting there. But he didn't think about coffins, what that is like. He didn't want to think about putting his mother in a box and the box in the ground and covering it with dirt, never to see her again. THESE ARE NOT NICE THINGS TO DO TO YOUR MOTHER. Not nice at all.

He wanted to die. He hoped to be run over or blown up. It was the least he could do. He secretly feared that his mother might need him in the after-life. He couldn't bear to think of her there having to cope all alone. The fact that she had been ill enough to die seemed a poor reason to abandon her.

He sat on sofas and thought: fifteen minutes ago I had fifteen minutes more life in me than I do now. It gave him hope, and helped to pass the time.

Disgust

He wanted to die, but couldn't. He couldn't bear to see Gail, couldn't bear to be touched. He felt no desire for SEX. Why would he want to nudge his favourite and most sensitive bodily part into someone else's intimate crevices and get himself all stinky and slimy and sweaty? WHO NEEDS THIS? He gave up his job for similar reasons, leaving his wretched colleagues nudging for promotion.

The Pacific islanders who were exiled to Mauritius, so that their own islands could be used for testing the atom bomb, died of ugliness. Mauritius was too ugly to bear. Robert too had seen ugliness, but so far it hadn't killed him. He was working on disgusting himself to death.

How Doris Day made it into the movies perplexed him. She had absolutely no sex appeal whatever. All that goody-goody housewife business. Aprons. She was kitsch! The terrible prudish innocence and vulnerability, the near-ugliness of her, especially her HAIR. It made him squirm.

Was Isabel anything like that? There was a fearful un-touchability about her. But he couldn't remember what he thought of Isabel. He felt nothing for anybody now. He was a broken man. And no one came to save him from this. They just told him to laugh at himself.

The only thing he found funny these days was the Evil Genius who plotted to destroy the world with a superbreed of influenza. 'Most people are filthy ignorant scum,' claimed the Evil Genius. 'I plan to destroy them all.'

Robert did not want to feel tender. Love meant having to take someone to the toilet. He thought with distaste of Isabel's boniness. His mother was old and bony. The thought of Isabel chilled him. Her stick-like legs and distended abdomen.

Humans are closely related to insects, he decided. We live and work in ghastly numbers and for some mysterious reason like ourselves enormously. Sloths, sharks, skunks – THESE can be individuals.

Out and About

Gail, in between frying other fish, occasionally tried to get Robert out and about. They arranged meetings, but he failed to turn up. The best way was to pick him up herself. She went to get him for a concert one day. She found him in front of the TV, as usual. But at least he'd switched it on. She considered that an improvement.

'You know, you really shouldn't spend so much time alone, Robert,' she said, surveying a multitude of discarded pizza cartons on the floor.

'Everybody lives in solitary confinement these days, Gail. Haven't you noticed? They only leave home for brief bouts of social contact and self-improvement. Scared of muggers, I guess.'

'I still say . . .' she said, authoritatively pursuing the subject of how one should live.

'Yeah, I know. There's a feeling going around that everybody's got to be HAPPY. If you're not, you've got to get up and do something to yourself. Get a shrink, get fresh air. Nobody's allowed their own tragedy any more. Sorrow is OUT.'

'Cheer up, Robert. You don't know what's around the corner.'

'I do know what's around the corner. What's around the corner is more of the same stuff. The only difference is, I don't plan to worry about it any more. I pity people who do.'

'Oh, come on, Robert. Get in the car and shut up.'

She had meant it fondly but Robert didn't appreciate being told to shut up. He was mute enough as it was – no one wanted to listen to any more of his feeble moaning. He sat glumly in the car as they drove through the streets he had travelled 6,000 miles to drive through.

He felt strange in the midst of the concert-hall crowd. There was a disgusting over-abundance of people in the world. And every man, woman and child was full of radiation. A woman in front of him sneezed. Everyone in the world has Strontium-90 in them, a radioisotope only produced by atomic explosions, and now I'm going to get that woman's cold as well! Some people have the conscience of an orang-utan. Why do they come to public places carrying infectious diseases? Why do they do this? But then he noticed that the despicable woman looked a little like his maternal grandmother, and he felt a pang of dismay that this forbear had also died on him at some point in his youth. Matrilineal deprivation, he thought, holding back tears.

The trio tuned up and played violently, with vile crescendos and desperate diminuendos. All music is violent and intrusive, thought Robert, violating the mind of the listener. It's a form of attention-seeking. He watched the girl ahead of him picking the ear-wax out of the ear of a man on her right. The guy could understand Schubert apparently, but not the rudiments of personal hygiene. It must be love. DISGUSTING. And the crescendos weren't crescendos. They were more like spontaneous fortissimos, and clearly startled the slumbering Japanese man beside Robert with their frenzy.

All the people around him were ugly. Watching TV can lead you to believe that the human race is generally good-looking. But here were people evidently afflicted with all kinds of deficiencies. During the intermission, he noticed a huge woman bedecked with turquoise who, despite the weight of herself and her jewellery, was boldly lunging for the leftover drinks at the bar and gulping them down.

On the wall of the men's room he noticed a machine selling 'The Night is Right' packets. These seemed to consist of three condoms, one toothbrush and two aspirin. Sounds like a great evening.

When he sat down again next to Gail, Robert was near explosion point. A couple settled themselves in the seat behind him, bumping Robert and momentarily encasing his head in a raincoat. The guy was expounding at length on his choice of running-shoe. The woman was bolstering him up with giggles and approbatory interjections.

Robert turned to them. 'If your conversation has to be so audible,' he said sweetly, 'could you make it a little more interesting? Because otherwise I will be forced to pray that your gonads turn cancerous.'

A Barren World

So there we leave Robert, a grown man brought down by
tragic circumstances. His only comfort: the moon face of his
mother in the sky every month.

Parents provide you with a sense of purpose, especially
sick ones, you should insist on that. Now that his mother
had embarked on her final disintegration, beyond his control, causing him to lose all sense of purpose, it might have
been more considerate of him to follow her example and
thereby save the world and himself any further thoughts on
the matter. But Robert has a fatal flaw, a mortal wound
that will keep him tottering about for another forty years or
so: he is hopeful. Beneath his present cynicism and despair,
as well as his acute state of disgust, lurk little flighty birds of
hope. He uncages them according to his capabilities, like
today he hopes merely to find the energy to go and buy
himself a hamburger. But with the aid of such high-protein
dinners, who knows what he will hope next?

He nurses and cherishes these feelings and curses the
world for its indifference to his slight improvement. You
drag yourself out of the desert desperate for water, and the
barman is busy. But this is not a romantic world. There's
not enough Santa Claus to go round. Everyone treats each
other with disdain. No one is indispensable. There are
mothers of twins who have trouble getting the buggy in

and out of shops. Who cares for these? There are people, our contemporaries, lost in libraries through the malice of evil librarians. Who loves these? We are all labouring under a lack of love, a bad situation for human beings. This situation is even bad for CATS.

The biggest threats to life now are leaky radiators, super-glue and pre-cooked chicken. When people were dying all over the place (Schubert just three months after declaring himself healthy), they lived with gusto. They did not waste a brushstroke because they feared death. But now people only die from their own or their doctor's negligence. Convinced of immortality, we're troubled by boredom, an inordinate sense of history and our own fecundity.

Animals have a much harder time of it. The world doesn't owe them a living. But at least they haven't forgotten what it's all about: you, the earth, the sky. Even trees know this.

The Happy Ending

While Robert was burying and subsequently missing his Mama, the Splendid Young Man was putting out feelers in California. He merely wished to make it clear that should there be a vacancy because of some teacher's prolonged absence or indifference, he himself would be happy to consider a lucrative position in Art History at Robert's university.

He had good reason to wish to leave the Catafalque. Cragshaw had disappeared without trace, only to be replaced by yet another Chardin scholar, Angelica Lotus had begun her year's paid maternity leave, Splutters had died of spontaneous combustion in a hotel room, and Pol was no longer amenable to any of the Splendid Young Man's devices, mechanical or otherwise. Sir Humphrey kept patting him on the bottom. Syms could see that he was in imminent danger of having to run the whole place single-handedly – the other hand held ready to fend off Basilisk and the hordes of blushing young females. Anyway, he fancied he might look even more splendid with a tan.

News of Lionel's new appointment dealt Robert a harsh blow. The guy was following him around the world, stealing his jobs. Robert needed help just to get through that day, but there was no one to help him. There was no hope. No mother, no lucrative job, no hope.

Luckily, a few more letters arrived in the mail that morning. One was from Isabel:

Dear Robert
   I was sorry to hear about your mother. I wish there was something I could do. I have had some troubled times myself since you left. To be frank, I miss you.

love,
Isabel

The other was from Pol:

ROBERT, As you never write, I can only assume that you're having a whale of a time over there, which heartily sickens me. I love you and want you over here. I mean it – come live with me by the sea. I've loved you for years. COME.

POL

Robert sold his house, split the money with Sandy, and set off for England to seek his fortune once more. But this time there would be a woman by his side.

   A woman who offered him everything, without even knowing how much he needed it.

   Miss Right.

The 34-year-old Woman in Limbo

I waited in vain to hear from Robert.

I expected some sort of cosmic sign to indicate that he had received my somewhat forward missive.

A slight earth tremor at the moment he opened it, travelling quickly across the globe to me in King's Cross, would not have gone amiss.

He lived on the San Andreas Fault after all.

This was my first love-letter.

I had bared my soul to him in that letter.

It made me weep to think of the vulnerability I had exposed to him.

But I wept partly from joy.

He would surely soon be here.

Perhaps he would just jump on a plane and come.

But then I worried about what would happen if he did come back to me.

The prospect of giving up the art of the unrequited passion was a daunting one.

I did not know if I could ever countenance any great amount of body contact either.

My person had always been inviolable.

The prospect of revealing to Robert all my physical defects was another daunting prospect.

The weird construction of my belly-button.

It was too embarrassing to contemplate.

Instead, I tried to concentrate on practicalities.

I reckoned my letter had a 70% chance of reaching Robert.

There was at least a 5% chance of its falling behind something at the Post Office and not getting to him for thirty years.

There was perhaps a 60–65% chance of its reaching him before he married that girl.

And then there was a 20% chance that he would want to come to ME.

Maybe 10%.

All in all, I estimated that there was about a 2% probability that he loved me, in the way that I loved him.

I wanted an equal relationship of that sort.

While I waited in limbo for my love, it was necessary to make interim plans.

Having completed her B.A. Honours degree in the History of Art, Pol was ready to move on.

Having been intensely miserable for some months, I had failed my finals.

So, without a degree, and without my love, it was now incumbent upon me to move out of Pol's flat.

We were not on particularly amiable terms by this time, although she had taken a kind interest in my decision to write to Robert.

Pol was going to live in Norfolk by the sea.

No doubt her layers of fat would be handy there against the east winds.

My mother and Alan, my step-father, did not seem overly keen to have me move in with them.

Ever since their fateful trip to Malta, they had suffered a revitalization of their sex life.

Disgusting though it may seem.

My mother now considered herself a liberated and sensual woman.

Awakened.

One night in Malta she was lying on a bed, while Alan was . . . doing his business.

She was watching a fan on the ceiling turning round and round.

This in some way electrified her.

In some way that I really did not wish to hear about.

At any rate, they now did not welcome intruders.

There was no place for me there.

Our Heroine's End

My hopes of making a fortune from that 'Chardin' relief painting had been dashed.

There was no sign of the thing in Dr Cragshaw's office.

I could not consult him about it either, for he had apparently come into some money and moved to Tahiti.

But I was to have a stroke of luck of my own.

One should never give up hope.

You never know what's round the corner.

Splutters, who had mysteriously passed away just after I had left him in a hotel room one day in a state (as usual) of some dishevelment, had given his country cottage to me in his will.

I was pleased.

More so perhaps than his wife.

I might have exciting excitements there, and learn about horse flesh.

All of Babs Cartwheel's heroines know about horse flesh.

With my spirits raised to a considerable degree, I set off for Suffolk.

There, Constable landscapes continually unfolded beneath me.

Art was the guiding force in my life.

The best that can be said for nature is that it occasionally looks like a painting.

One day, longing for Robert, I wandered lonely as a Constable cloud into the middle of a field of poppies.

The colour was magnificent.

Especially when compared to my own.

I thought of their little lives, more daring and exciting than my own.

And I fell asleep.

It is hard to die usually, but for me it was easy.

I lay sleeping there in the poppy field.

A rash developed all over my body.

I sank into a coma.

No one came to rouse me.

No one came to rescue me, as I lay in a sea of undulating waves of grass, surging over me.

No one came to cure my coma by talking to me and playing my favourite Frank Sinatra records over and over night and day for months until at last a flickering eyelid or hand movement assured them that my coma was lifting, to their eternal joy.

I have always dreaded depending on the benevolence of others.

It would be terrible to grow old and increasingly allergic to bee-stings.

What if they forgot about your anti-bee-sting injection?

There you'd be, wheeled out in your bath-chair to enjoy the fresh air and bzzz – that would be the end of you.

My end was actually quite quick.

For, along with nuts and bees, I am extremely allergic to poppy seeds.

I had always avoided opium for this reason.

I died as I had lived.

I never gave up hope.

I never settled for second-best.

Even throughout my strange dallying with Splutters, I had saved myself for Robert.

Our love was divine.

God spared me the knowledge, therefore, that Robert preferred Pol, the devil he knew.

'Donuts Ex Machina'

Isabel exaggerates. She did not go into a coma. Feeling fine after her sleep in the poppy field, she took a bus to Sudbury to buy some groceries. There she met her father, who ran a donut shop. He instantly recognized her, and was so pleased to see her that he offered her a job as a walking donut, advertising his bakery. From this she derived her idea of Personal Space.

She also learned from him the bare facts of her birth, which clarified many things for her. She realized she was genetically predisposed to Rape Fantasies, and from then on she no longer mourned her body, or doubted its readiness and worthiness for the purposes of love. Her knobbly knees and crooked toes. Her unpredictable hair. They would all do in the end.

Personal Space

I became an artist of Personal Space.

Personal Space is the space that exists between different parts of the body.

For instance, there is a triangular space from one's ear to one's shoulder.

There is a much larger expanse of personal territory between the nose and the toes of a standing person.

An intrusion on these spaces by a stranger incurs hostility.

Hence one's reluctance to travel in crowded trains.

Hence one's aversion to crowds of all kinds.

And to being touched without due respect for one's personal spaces.

I became a performance artist, performing demonstrations of my theory of Personal Space.

I was much in demand at the ICA.

_large area
of
Personal Space_

triangular area

_Additional spherical area,
achieved by
artificial means
(donut costume)_

Yet Another Ending (In Which Nobody Dies)

Robert returned from America a wiser man, with a tan, and married Isabel. They made a very imperfect couple and lived happily ever after in the country cottage, where Robert wrote books on the sublime and Isabel carried on with her performance art. He never admitted how silly he found her work; she never mentioned how romantic she found his. Her thinness troubled him. Her bones reminded him of death. She was physical evidence for him of the flimsiness and fallibility of the construction that makes a living, breathing, talking, walking companion. While he liked her arms when bent, the abdomen seemed to him a land of no return, a vast plain.

He hitched a dog to his sled and slid out across the Alaskan wilderness, his new-found land. He wondered if he was becoming too involved with people again. He had to draw back a bit. He pulled in the dog-sled and settled down for the night, leaving the great frozen interior bare as far as the eye could see. They were like two people clinging in the snow. His polar vision chilled her.

He saw Pol whenever he could get away. He needed to be by the sea, near an end to humanity.

The Beginning of the End

And Angelica Lotus had her baby – $10\frac{1}{2}$ lbs – her cushion
to lie on and plump up for the rest of her life, her lonely
life.

The Whole History of My Life

Lucy Ellmann was born in Evanston, Illinois, also the birth-place of the hot-dog. She was dragged to England against her better judgement at the tender and formative age of thirteen. She proceeded to go into a decline, which still continues. She has worked as a selector of music to accompany the test screen on BBC2, before moving on to a similar post at Channel 4. This was her only method of communicating with the outside world for some ten years. All fan mail welcome.